THE MOTH
AND OTHER TANTALIZING TALES

JAMES L HILL

Twisted Christmas was first published in Tis The Season: A Holiday Anthology: 2020 Season (2020)

The Path to Freedom was first published in Dark Corners of the Old Dominion: A Virginia Horrors Anthology (2023)

Thanks to Athina Paris, Editor, for her dedication and tireless effort.

Published By

RockHill Publishing LLC

PO Box 62241

Virginia Beach, VA 23466-2241

www.rockhillpublishing.com

CONTENTS

COLD STORAGE

My name is Paul Michael Smith, and I am the oldest man to have ever lived. Someone once said longevity is a blessing. However, I can attest to the fact that when your blessings are manufactured in a lab, life becomes pain, misery, and sorrow.

I was a happy kid, my mother and father loved me, I had lots of friends at school. I was smart, smarter than most six-year-olds. No. "Prideful thinking leads to the Devil's punishment," that's what my grandma always said. And perhaps that's what happened to me. But to tell the truth, I don't know where the monster came from. I do know when I first saw him.

It was a crisp autumn day. I threw my jacket on the pile and ran to join the kickball game. Big Jimmy was blocking the net, but I kept running as hard as I could. I caught up to the ball just in time to kick it right at Jimmy. Jimmy was big but he couldn't catch. The ball bounced off Big Jimmy and hit me right in the face, so fast I didn't have time to blink. I woke up with a black eye, bloody nose, and a bad headache in the hospital. My mother was crying. My father was arguing with the doctor. He didn't want me to remain in the hospital. But I did remain in the hospital that day and that year. Dr. Adams told me I had more than just a bloody nose and a black eye. I had leukemia. I had cancer.

He told me, "It is a monster that wants your strength. If we work really hard we can put that monster in the closet and lock the door."

Every place he stuck his needles drained the monster from my body. The monster took some of me into the closet too. When he got loose, he was bigger, stronger, and more painful. Just when I thought I could go out to play, or my hair looked good, or I could eat without puking, the monster got out. And Dr. Adams' needles and machines would go to work putting the monster back in the closet.

During my time in the hospital, I would draw. Everyone loved my pictures. "Such depth... What beauty... Awesome..." My black and whites were especially praised, and it wasn't long before they were selling. I wanted to believe they were that good, but you know prideful thinking. I was in the hospital so much my mother and father often forgot when I was home. I could hear them fighting about the money. The pictures helped, but not enough. The experimental drugs cost more than what my pictures sold for.

One day, during an argument, my father said, "The next time, we should refuse treatment. We can do that, you know. He's fifteen and what has he got to show for a life, a room full of drawings, and a life full of pain. We can refuse treatment."

On TV there were others who felt like my father, they called themselves the Moral Right. They were against medical experiments, stem cell treatment which kept me alive, and DNA manipulation. They were fighting for Death with Dignity. What my father was planning scared the monster deep into the closet. The monster knew that when I died, he died. So, he stayed in his closet.

People like art because they can see what they want in it.

Art is the reflection of the viewer not the artist. My work was acclaimed as fresh, realism in a surrealistic world, and the ever-popular awe-inspiring. My pain was inspiring. My despair was uplifting. I was 'IT' from New York to LA. Being an artist wasn't so hard, couple of black lines on a paper, some gray dust from the graves of the less fortunate, a ghostly picture of some passing friend and I was a success. People enjoyed the misery. My greatest work was a huge 18 by 12-foot canvas. It was like the others, lines of various shades of death crisscrossing and intersecting at random points of misery. Mom said it was like looking out of an ice cube. I wrote in tiny letters down in the corner, 'Life in Ice'. It was the only piece I put a title on. It attracted Dr. Leonardo Targue to MOCA, the Museum of Contemporary Art in Los Angeles.

Dr. Targue wanted to make Life in Ice more than a conceptual dream; he planned to make it a reality for me. Yes, Dr. Leonardo Targue was a cryogenic scientist. He was different from the other doctors. He offered no cure, he gave no false hope of a miracle, he suggested escape from the monster. The monster hated him. He smashed the closet door and poured misery into my soul the day I met Dr. Targue. The only thing that hated Dr. Targue more was the Moral Right. They despised the doctor, scientists, and anyone who challenged God's domain or will.

Although cryogenics wasn't a new technology, Dr. Targue was taking a novel, controversial, and potentially illegal approach to it. Conventional cryo-doctors froze you moments after you died with the hope that someone would be able to bring you back to life. The good doctor Targue planned to freeze me while I was alive and relatively healthy. He also did his colleagues one better, he actually had a process for reanimation.

Because I would be alive when I underwent his cryogenic procedure; the whole thing was top secret.

October 4th, the day I turned 21, "the day Janis Joplin died," remarked Dr. Targue, was the day I met him at his prep facility. He administered chemo for my leukemia and his frog serum for the cryo. The frog serum was a combination of fluids that allowed reptiles to survive cold temperature and hibernation. He was going to infuse my body with it to protect my cells during the freezing phase. It was also an electrolyte that would allow my cells to be reactivated with low voltage energy. I had the feeling he had tried this before; I couldn't tell if he had been successful.

"Imagine how science, how medicine will change when I freeze you and bring you back whole." I imagined the Moral Right coming after him with pitchforks and torches. They didn't like frozen embryos, they would scream "crucify him," over Popsicle people. I was sedated for the trip to the secret cryogenic lab.

'Piece of my heart' was pounding in my ears. The stark white sparsely adorned lab was more sterile than any hospital I had ever seen. Dr. Targue pulled me from the blue gel-filled bathtub. I took a second look around at some white leather couches, a computer desk, a wall of electronic equipment, and no windows. The doctor lowered the sorrowful sounds of Janis Joplin and told me I'd been in the steel cryotub for three days.

Other than feeling sticky all over from the blue gel I was fine. The electric shock process to restart my body destroyed the frog juice as well. "This is not like being asleep, no dreams and no sense of waking up. It's like getting hit in the face by the red kickball, and then wham, nothingness," I informed the doctor.

Two days later the monster was loose again, angrier than ever, the white flowing spectra racing through my body, his fiery eyes cooking my insides and his needle teeth pricking every single nerve. Agony spewed from my mouth in buckets of black bile. The monster didn't like the nothingness. In the closet he was still there, I could feel him, but in cryo we didn't exist. I couldn't wait to get back. Next, Dr. Targue put me in an exo-skin to monitor my vital signs while I spent a year in cryo. "I thought I wouldn't exhibit any signs."

"That is correct," he confirmed, "but if your body's temperature fluctuates, or if there is any brain activity then there is a problem. I'll need to reanimate you immediately. Also, the exo-skin has micro electrodes to stimulate your entire body during reanimation."

We talked at length; the doctor was worried that the Moral Right was gaining an advantage in the government. Once again science and religion were at odds. I plugged the wire harness into the receptacle just about the gel line. I floated, suspended in the gel. The doctor closed the lid. The darkness was total. The next second, the gel froze, not hard or stiff, just frozen. I was back into the Nothingness.

Janis was screaming in soulful misery. The emptiness of the lab was vividly clear. I climbed out of the nothingness back into the world. Dr. Targue was calling me, "Paul, come to the communication panel."

I stood before the huge monitor with blue gel dripping on the white tiles. "Is the year up? Where are you?" The scene panned out and I realized Dr. Targue was in a courtroom. He was on trial. A dozen people were shouting at each other, the doctor, and me. I learned it had been three years and the doctor was facing a litany of charges from murder to crimes against human-ity. He would beat the murder charges since I was alive but publishing his research on cryogenics left him with plenty of others. I testified that I had no knowledge of where I was, no intention of leaving the lab, and bore no ill will towards the good doctor. I ended the communication with a farewell to the doctor. "I look forward to cryo and a world when my monster can finally be put to death. Doc, revive me when that is possible. Good luck and thanks for all that you've done for me."

~

'Me and Bobby McGee' greeted me along with a very young girl in a lab coat. "What year is it?"

"3506-10-04," she told me, "It's your birthday."

"Of course it is," I responded. In the nothingness time had no meaning. Fifteen hundred years, give or take, was but a fleeting moment for me. I had just turned twenty-five. I realized that I was not in Dr. Targue's lab. This was some kind of hospital – even though I didn't recognize any of the equipment, I recognized the look. I gave her a good look too. She was just a kid. "You work here?"

"Yes. I'm Eylene, the researcher who led the team that retrieved you from the desert."

I bluntly asked, "How old are you?"

"Twelve," she said proudly, "I have been a researcher for three years now. I've dedicated my life to finding you."

"Why? Have you found a cure for cancer? Where are the real doctors?"

"Cancer was eradicated more than four hundred years ago. But it came at an expense no one could have foreseen. After they cleaned the environment, most cancers disappeared. The last ones were genetic in nature, like yours."

So, they had gone ahead with genetic manipulation of the population. The fix had dire consequences, people started dying younger. The mortality rate dropped from a hundred years on average to eighty in the generation after the mod. And in each successive generation it continued to fall. Now, the average life-span was twenty-five years. Couple that with a plummeting birthrate, less than ten percent of the population conceived, and because thirteen was the average age of first-time mothers, only a third survived.

"Less than one percent of the population has more than one child," Eylene said sadly, "that's why we need you to reintroduce the cancer gene back into the populace."

"But you can cure me, right?"

"The cure for cancer has always been death," she said coldly. "I studied Doctor Targue's records. He was very clever hiding his cryolab under the Pyramids of Giza. However, he left no notes on how his cryofluids were made. You are the only one we could reanimate from your era because you're the only one who went into cryogenic storage alive. We will begin making the genetic serum as soon as the cancer has returned."

They made their serum from my marrow. Injected it into pre-teenagers and waited for results. Even though the monster had returned in full force I did not feel him. The fire was quenched by nanobots, millions of them roaming through my body. They didn't need the frog juice to return me to cryo either, another group of bots produced the hibernating fluids and froze it at the cellular level. No cryotub, no blue gel, just wham into the nothingness again, the monster and me.

I returned ten years later to see Eylene haggard and worn. There was no music playing. I was in an isolation chamber suspended by hair-thin wires and tubes. Millions of them connected me to the ceiling, walls, and floor of the chamber. Eylene had had three miscarriages before the serum rendered her infertile. All the girls who took the serum had miscarriages or stillbirths. The boys who fathered children with non-treated girls, their offspring lived, but none past a decade. And the boys died before their twenties.

I was being prepared for the next series of sera to be given to the boys only. When it was done, I was returned to the cryo-state, back to the nothingness. I was reanimated again twenty-five years later. A generation of serum babies were born, reached puberty, and had children. Most of the second generation died in early child-hood. Humanity was on the brink of extinction. There were far too few to go on. They were going to make a serum from my blood and the healthy supply they had stored up over the years. They planned to give it to everyone, no matter what age or gender. Either humanity would rise from the sea of sorrows or it would be lost for all time. My only request was, "Am I allowed to die with dignity?"

The wall in front of my bed cleared and sunshine bathed my boney body for the first time in centuries. A marble statue a hundred feet tall stood in the courtyard. I finally recognized the monster, the true monster, a doctor with test tubes and beakers trying to beat God.

THE END

ANTIBODY

2 9 May 2029. THE TRUTH BE TOLD. *vincit omnia veritas* (truth conquers all things).

They are at it again. Who are they? The powers that be. What are they up to this time? Unless you have been in a coma for the last decade, or living under a rock, which I seriously doubt, because in the past ten years THEY have left no stone unturned. Nor freedom untrampled.

First, THEY unleashed the plague. I know, there are some who still believe it was a natural occurrence, an Act of God (for my End of the World friends), an accident (some buttered-fingers, overworked, underpaid, lab rat – human or actual furry creature) that innocently infected the world with COVID-19. The fact remains, well over 3 million people died in 2020.

The video screen segmented, and the annoying beep-bloop-blots repeated in a form of a robotic tune accompanied the picture of Vincent Meyer, his royal-blue silk pajama top hanging open down his chest.

Baron shook his head wearily. "What is it, Vincent?"

"Your girlfriend is back," Vincent said with a twisted

smile, "she dropped about a million words manifesto on the worldwide conspiracy network. Have you seen it?"

"I was just getting to it, and she IS NOT MY GIRLFRIEND."

"Hey, easy, old man," Vincent said, and smacked a young topless girl on her bottom as she passed by the camera. "Daddy's working, sweetie. Go put something on before you give my friend here a heart attack, or something worse."

The young woman stopped, looked into the screen wide-eyed, and waved, then scooted out of the picture.

Baron stroked his short, black beard and tried to hide his pleasure. "If you were her daddy, she would be about six. She looks older than that to me. I am sure you read the whole thing already, why don't you give me the long and short of it."

Vincent walked over to his desk and the camera followed him. The window behind him was blue and white, fluffy clouds hanging over his shoulder.

He sipped from a whiskey glass as he tapped the virtual keyboard on his desk. "Ah, here it is. Let's see… People died 2020. More people died 2021. Vaccine is a hoax, no long-term cure, more of her greatest hits. Here's something new," he looked up from the screen embedded in the black oak. "She is accusing President Harris of killing President Biden. Oh, no, wait," a finger shot up in the air as he scanned the screen more carefully, "your girlfriend, Veritas, is accusing Harris of covering up the fact that Biden died back in October of 22 from MOFASD. A full two years before anyone knew of the new variant that caused it."

Baron returned from the kitchen with a glass of orange juice in his hand. His tattered and very comfortable tee-shirt hung loosely around his rounding belly. He hadn't become fat as of yet, but he was losing the battle of the bulge that came to a man in his forties. He considered himself lucky this day, as another totally nude woman, a short-haired brunette crossed between the camera and his friend. Ordinarily, he would not have noticed her hair color, but the curtains matched the carpet, unusual for the supermodel types. "How does Veritas claim to know Biden died from 'Major Organ Failure And Sudden Death' in October and not of a simple heart attack in December of 22 like it was reported?"

"Orange Juice. What time is it in, ummm…"

"I'm in Norfolk," Baron huffed, "and it's just past 7 am."

Baron Beard was always annoyed that this young techie was sailing around the world on his— who knew—billion-dollar yacht and didn't even give a second thought to the plight or the lives of the rest of humanity. He was just like all the other uber rich asses, whom, as soon as the virus struck, cashed in on it, and got the Hell out of Dodge. Whether it was mega-yachts, private islands, or palatial estates well-hidden and secluded, the rich did not suffer the effects of Covid-19. "Well, Veritas dropped the C word right in the beginning, so I am sure this blog is going to be obliterated before more than a handful of us get to read it. She used to be more careful about things like that, I guess going dark for three years makes one a little rusty. Hey, where are you anyway?"

"I don't know, really," Vincent smirked. He loved to rub his wealth in Baron's face.

He had met him at the university and taken his journalism class. Baron was one of those passionate types, all hyped-up about his fellow man and justice. Vincent enjoyed the hours of debates, and the torture he subjected Baron to as he told him how technology was going to make him very, very, very rich. And it did. Vincent argued technology was going to level the playing fields for the Blackman. Invent something, put your stamp on it, and sell it to the world. He told Baron he'd be filthy rich before anyone even knew his name, and he was right. He wasn't gung-ho for affirmative action, but he was just a click shy of fist in the air, black power. Until he made his money and shifted from we-got-to take-power, to I-made-it-to-Hell-with-the-rest.

"We left my island in the Seychelles a couple days ago. Had to pick up a couple of new toys. You know what I mean."

"You better be careful you don't pick up more than you bargained for." Baron truly hoped he didn't.

Vincent was an insufferable pain in the ass, but he was a nice guy, and Baron needed that big brain of his. Vincent was half innovator and half hacker. He had developed some of the most sophisticated software for the government, and stole the rest. He was also a good, if not great engineer. His biotech was the envy of the 21st century. But it was in telecommunication where he really excelled. The Covid lockdown was like a goldmine to him. He dug deep and fast.

"What makes Veritas think Biden died from MOFASD? And three months before anyone knew he was dead?"

"She hints at uncovering body double footage, time discrepancies, and flat-out deep fakes," Vincent looked hard into the camera for a long time before continuing, "here's why I'm calling you this early in the morning. I sat on this for a few hours, waiting for you to roll out of bed. I tracked one of the servers she used to Chicago. And if you hurry, you can pick up your girlfriend's trail before it goes dark."

"I don't know why you insist on calling her my girlfriend, I don't believe Veritas is a woman. I believe it's a cover, she writes like a he, and what the hell! I'm not going to Chicago, it's a damn Red Zone. And I couldn't get in there even if I wanted to," Baron gulped down his OJ and cleared his throat, "which I don't." He walked off the camera and returned chewing a piece of toast. "Veritas is too good to be caught using a cat cable to upload her work."

Vincent waved to someone off camera then smiled a big silly grin, "that is what I thought, but it's a server in a protected farm, it only sends information out. It's in the Medical Records Office, which means she either works there or knows someone who does. And as for Chicago being a Red Zone, those zones are designed to keep people in, not out like the Green Zones. There is an Autodriver waiting for you outside, it will take you into Hammond, Indiana, a Yellow Zone. From there I will get you into Chicago." He held up his hand to someone off camera. "Hey, the girls are getting restless. They will start without me in a minute. Everything you need is in the Autodriver. What was the saying from that old TV show? 'The truth is out there.' Go get'em."

∾

Baron walked out the door of his house around noon and into the sweltering heat of a mid-May's day. Sweat beads immediately formed on his arms and trickled down the backs of his hands.

Too damn hot. Shouldn't be this hot in May. Whatever happened to the Green New Deal fixing the climate? Oh yeah, that was bullshit!

The black-out SUV sat in his driveway behind his '92 Dodge Viper, which he washed and polished weekly, although he could never drive it. He had bought it for a steal at two hundred thousand dollars in 2025, four times the original price and one-fifteenth of its top price before Covid and the gasoline restrictions. His neighbors asked why he didn't keep it in his garage, he answered, "I bought it so people could see it."

The black SUV Autodriver dwarfed his sports car, it was nothing like the four-seater little electric razor-type the auto industries started putting out in 2025. Like every other business, the automobile manufacturers fell victims to the deadly two-punch of climate science and covid restrictions. Nobody was buying electric vehicles, EVs as they were branded to make them sound desirable, and they kept getting smaller and less attractive over the three years that they were mandated. Then the government shut down gasoline sales to the public in 2025, and every car became obsolete overnight. That was when Baron bought his

Viper, his dream car. He sat behind the wheel in his driveway, imagining himself flying down the highway, blasting Rush's Red Barchetta on the radio. He laughed, as he knew his neighbors thought he had lost his mind.

The SUV door opened to reveal an immaculate interior. He had hoped Vincent included a little company for the long drive, but no such luck. He threw his small black overnight bag on the far side leather seat. He climbed in with a small shoulder bag on his back. The door slid closed, and he made himself comfortable on the back seat. He opened the concertina doors of the bar in the center of the van and looked over the selection of liquors.

"It's about time you showed up," Vincent's voice filled the van. "I did say you should try and catch Veritas before she goes dark again."

The lights on the dashboard came on and the low whine of the electric engine momentarily made itself known. A feature added to the self-driving electric vehicles as some people stepped out of them not realizing they were in motion.

"You will be happy to know the SUV checked the air and no sign of the corona virus or any of its variants has been detected." Another feature added as the Zones went into effect. Vincent continued. "You have a clean bill of health."

"Considering I haven't been any further than my driveway in years, I didn't think I had anything to worry about. The bout I had with Covid was six years ago now, and I never had any of those lingering symptoms people complained about."

"Why are you packing the hardware?" Vincent's face appeared on the monitor that folded down from the SUV's ceiling. "There is a built-in magnetometer."

"That's something you don't get on your run-of-the-mill, factory standard, Autodriver."

"This baby is packed with a lot of bells and whistles," Vincent sat on the back of his yacht surrounded by trays of food.

"For example, I can tell you have three guns in your bag, but only, maybe, fifty rounds of ammunition."

"You're the one sending me into an F'ing Red Zone," Baron did not believe in cussing, "I just want to make sure I get out."

"But only fifty rounds…"

"Hey, I'm not blowing a year's supply on one wild-goose chase," Baron looked around the SUV cabin for other hidden devices. "Besides, people will kill you these days just for your ammo. A couple of mags is all I need to encouraged people to get out of my way."

Vincent wiped his mouth and drank a glass of champagne. He always ate alone. "Look in the compartment under the back seat. There's a little something for your safety in there."

Baron pressed the panel in and it folded out between his legs. There were two black and red guns in holsters. The pistols were smaller than his Smith & Wesson 9mm. He pulled it out and was turning it over, looking for the magazine ejection button.

"You can stop looking for how to load it," Vincent told him, "It is an ionic magnetic pulse gun. You know, a stun gun without the pesky wires."

"A freaking stun gun," Baron shouted at the screen, "you want me to go to Chicago with a freaking bug zapper. Are you out of your mind? Even before all this crazy Covid shit, I wouldn't go to Chicago without some serious heat. I'm not giving up my S&W, Beretta, or my MP5 for a zapper."

"You have an MP5, a submachine gun? Aren't they illegal?"

"Only if you shoot somebody."

Vincent laughed. "That bug zapper has two settings. Flip the safety down and it fires a plasma charge capable of knocking a three-hundred-pound man in full protective gear out cold at three hundred yards. Flip it up and you send him to the morgue. And you don't have to worry about running out of bullets, it fires over ten thousand times at three milliseconds intervals before it needs recharging. I guarantee you'll be able to walk out of Kabul with that in hand."

"I'm guessing this isn't legal either?"

"Not once you pull the trigger. Now, his big brother down there will stop a tank at about ten miles. Best thing about these weapons is once they are paired to your biorhythms, only you can fire them. And you must be alive and awake to do so. None of that cutting off your hands and making a glove out of it that plagued the army's direct energy weaponry."

"Good to know. I hope that selling point was well advertised."

"Are you kidding me? None of this is out in public, not the military, nowhere. Only my personal security detail has them, so please, don't lose it." The seriousness of the last statement turned his ever-present smile to a scowl. He looked around cautiously before continuing, "when you press the trigger the gun's laser targeting determines the range and calculates the strength of the magnetic containment field for the ionized gas which it pulls in from the surrounding atmosphere. At low energy, the gas plasma is about the size of a grain of rice, at high power, a pea. At any rate, it moves at near the speed of light, so your target, or anyone else, won't see it coming. The rifle on the other hand, fires a much larger pulse and at a slower speed. It is somewhat visible over distance, so use it only in the direst of circumstances. If either of these weapons get away from you, they will self-destruct in a spectacular fashion." His smile returned as he seemed pleased with the warning.

Baron watched the iron barricades roll back as he approached the Hampton Roads Bridge and Tunnel which was the quickest way out of Norfolk. The Autodriver slowed to 70 mph as it passed the fortified checkpoint, the first of many. He was surprised the vehicle did not have to stop, then realized his trip was preapproved. It slowed down for the necessary scans, to confirm he was the only passenger. The virus and subsequent zonings made travelling anywhere almost impossible. All inter-state travel had to be approved weeks in advance by the Department of Transportation. Baron wondered how Vincent had got this trip okayed in a day.

"Hey, one more present for you," Vincent read the signs of concern on his friend's face and decided to curtail any questions he was about to ask. "This is the most important piece of equipment I could provide."

"What is it? A teleporter? Are you about to beam me up, Scotty?"

"Ha ha ha. I wish I could." Vincent's fake laugh did not hide the secrecy of what he was about to reveal. "Inside the console is a foil pouch, inside it is an ectoskin. Put it on."

Baron found the pouch, opened it, and looked inside. He saw two strips of ribbon, one red, and the other green. "Hey! I think you've been robbed. There's nothing in here but the price tags."

"Not the price tags my technically challenged friend. The suit is a one-piece, ultra-fine mesh material which is invisible under any light. The red and green stripes are the only way you can find it when you are not wearing it. It will block any microbes from entering or leaving your body."

Baron grabbed the two stripes and touched the softest material he had ever felt between his fingers. He pulled it out of the pouch and felt arms and legs even though he saw nothing. Judging from the length of the material he figured it to be made for a child, a toddler at best. "You are kidding, right? Am I supposed to fit in this?"

"It's super stretchy, with a full body hoody. You know, like the pajamas the girls like to wear. You step in first, put your arms in, and pull the hood over your head. The red and green stripes will disappear, and you will be completely sealed inside. Don't take it off for any reason unless you are in the SUV."

"How am I supposed to eat," Baron smirked, "and, you know, do other things?"

"Air and liquids pass through without a hitch. Solids are a problem, as you can image. The ectoskin is powered by your body's heat and kills microbes on contact. My people tell me it makes anything you drink taste funny. Gives it a slight metallic taste. A small price to pay to protect against G.1.927.2, or as you news people like to call it, The Herod Variant, because it killed children."

Baron found the button on the bottom of the video screen and switched off the camera. He slipped on the ectoskin with surprising ease. He took a couple of test breaths and felt no strange effects. It was completely form-fitting, molding to his fingers and toes, and every other part of his body. Within seconds he forgot he had it on. He dressed and switched back on the camera. "How durable is this stuff?"

"You can shower in it. Scrub with it on. But don't think it's bulletproof, or gas proof, it will not protect you from anything other than biological entities. Well, that's all I got for you. I'll check in when you get to Indiana."

The long ride to Indiana gave Baron time to read the entire 'The Truth Be Told' message. He chuckled at the part about the lawmakers being too afraid to take people's guns away, so they outlawed the ammunition. He had beaten Veritas to the point a year ahead of her conspiracy theory. In his article, 'The Vanishing Bullet', he stated the rise in mass shootings and the J6 Insurrection had made it easy for Congress to put limits on the manufacturing of ammunition. Then as part of a massive bill in 2022, they limited the number of bullets a person could buy to one hundred rounds every three months. The Republicans raged against the bill, as they did against most of the laws passed after

'22, but they lost handily in that election cycle, and the Dems were making them pay. The Republicans privately supported the bill and many others after the J6 Insurrection as the only way to keep themselves safe.

The Dems pushed through the Green New Deal legislation. Veritas claimed it was the main reason Harris covered up Biden's death. If the country knew she was the President, the '22 elections might have swung the other way. She claimed Biden's speeches were taped, or given by his body double, or cobbled together from other sources. The fact that he gave so few speeches was her proof he died long before anybody knew it.

Baron considered Veritas a conspiracy theorist, much like Q, or the Red Letter, or a half-dozen other crazies on the internet. But Veritas' theories usually came true, if not when announced, not too long afterward. He on the other hand was a serious journalist. He named sources when he could, gathered facts and supporting evidence before printing his findings. He revisited his disappearing bullets story when the Green New Deal made copper a high-demand resource, and therefore not available for brass bullet casting.

To make it easier for people to switch to electric vehicles, the Federal Government started putting in charging strips on the interstate highways. All electric cars had a charging inducer built-in like in your phone. As one drove over the five-mile sections in the highway, the car's battery would fully charge. That killed the argument that an electric car could not be used for long-distance travel. It also meant no one had to pay for the power. There were debates about tolls but in the end the electric grid was free to all.

As Baron had written in one of his columns, "The gates to Utopia are about to swing wide open. Travel across America, free and unrestricted, will usher in a new spirit of brotherhood as we climb out of the shadow of Covid-19 isolation." As the SUV quietly rolled over the red and yellow stripes of a charging section, he thought, *how could I have been so wrong?*

He wasn't to blame for the miscalculation, although, over the years, he was the focus. MOFASD exploded on the scene in July 2023. People, otherwise healthy and without warning, were having massive killer heart attacks. Others suffered renal failure and died where they stood. Baron reported that people woke up unable to urinate, then noticed swelling in their legs, ankles, and feet. By nightfall, they developed muscle twitching, itching, and drowsiness. From there, it was seizures or a brief comatose state, and death.

In October of '23, days after Veritas released a memo from the CDC of the alarming numbers of deaths from Acute Liver Failure among young non-alcohol abusers, Baron ran the numbers and found shockingly, the one thing all these people had in common was Covid-19. The heart attacks, the kidney failures, and the liver failure victims all had traces of a new variant, Gamma. Veritas accused the CDC and the government of covering up the facts. Hiding the numbers by reporting each death from a failure as if it were unrelated to the others by virtue of being a different organ in the body.

Baron could see how the government could miss it. Some people had been vaccinated. All showed no signs of sickness. And he surmised, things were starting to get back to normal, no one wanted to go back to Covid life. But around the world, this new variant was taking hold and killing on a scale that was, even by Covid standards, unprecedented. When he looked at the numbers worldwide, sixty-two thousand a day were dying. He wrote of his findings, "the world is doing a twostep of death with Covid. One step forward and two steps back into a shallow grave."

He caught flack for that statement, but it was true. Later reporting showed the Gamma variant took twenty-four hours or less to reach contagion or viral-shed levels, was undetectable except via blood testing, and death followed within seven to ten days. With the last day being the only day, anyone knew they were sick. In the same column, he urged the Harris administration to return to lockdown measures immediately. She did not.

Veritas was less subtle in her missive. 15November2023. THE TRUTH BE TOLD. *vincit omnia veritas* (truth conquers all things).

Harris was following the playbook of Trump, pretending everything was just fine and dandy, while silencing the doctors and scientists to win re-election. It did not go well for him; it would not end well for her. This lie would all but ensure his return.

However, no one knew what the lie she was speaking of was then. And she never explained her post afterwards as she so often did when the truth came out. Those few words were the last she wrote for a few years.

But Harris got the message, she announced a 'Build the Wall' campaign of her own on both borders to stop people infected with Covid from entering the United States. It effectively cut the legs out from under Trump and any other Republican seeking the office. She easily won re-election with, "Build the Wall in '24. Make it safe for all."

Baron felt the SUV slow down. He was approaching the Indiana state line. The Welcome sign was riddled with bullet holes from the battle four years ago when a group of three thousand people tried to run the barricades. With tanks and armored vehicles across the highway they had no chance of succeeding. It took seven hours and dozens of deaths before the 'Free Indianans' turned around and went home.

Since then, steel drawbridges have been installed at every state line by the federal government. The secondary roads were still manned by the National Guard, however, few people tried to travel farther than allowed. Once the Interstate Zoning Law went into effect, gasoline sales were restricted to five gallons per day. People realized they couldn't get far on so little gas, and no matter where they were going, Covid was waiting for them.

Travel was restricted to medical personnel, active-duty military, and with special clearance from the Department of Transportation, journalists. Baron had worked from home for the past three years, telecommunicating with interviewees, and downloading documentation over secure servers. The last major trip he took was in 2026 to the United Nations in New York City. That was when all nations agreed to close their borders and banned all international flights.

Covid had won.

The SUV stopped and Baron lowered the window for his viral scan. A soldier in a hazmat suit approached with his M16 hanging down his right side and the black biological kit in his left hand. He held the small cube up to the window and said, "Eyes wide open, look into the red light."

"Yes, sir," Baron replied and stared at the bright red dot in the footlong rectangular slit. He had been through many of these medical scans.

The soldier read the display screen on the back of the cube and set it on the ground. He flipped two latches on the right side and folded back the top section. He pulled a nose cup with a long clear tube out and handed it to Baron. It looked exactly like the oxygen mask flight attendants used to demonstrate emergency procedures on planes when people were allowed to fly.

"Is that thing clean?" Baron joked.

The soldier behind his clear face-shield kept his stern visage, "take a deep breath in, then exhale hard."

Baron followed instructions. He inhaled the cold lemon-scented gas, which he was sure was not just air and blew out as hard as he could. The machine pulled more air from his lungs than he thought he had, causing a burning sensation. He hated the lung scan test.

The machine started beeping and flashing red on the screen display.

The soldier stepped back and snapped his weapon to the ready position. "Mr. Donald Dreiser, please step out of the vehicle with your hands up!"

"Wait! No! There must be a mistake," Baron objected. His heart rate jumped incredibly high. "That machine is wrong; my name isn't Don… what did you call me?"

"You have tested positive for Covid-19 virus," the soldier's finger was steady on the trigger. The harshness of his words came through the plastic face-shield loud and strong. "Are you admitting to travelling under a falsified identity in violation of section 2.42 of the U.S. Interstate Zoning Code? A crime which gives me the authority to immediately employ lethal force to stop you from going any farther."

Before Baron could answer, four more soldiers took positions around the SUV.

God damn you, Vincent, what have you got me into? "No. That is not what I am saying. I am Don Dryer. I am saying, I don't have Covid-19. I haven't had it for more than eight years. I have been vaccinated and get my regular semi-annual boosters. That machine is wrong! It is reading a false positive."

"Step out of the vehicle, slowly. Put your hands on your head. Or I will shoot."

Baron pressed the door button, and it slid to the rear. He carefully placed both hands on his head, his feet on the ground, and stood up very slowly.

A fifth soldier exited the guard station wearing what looked like flamethrower equipment.

Baron had seen what was about to happen to him on television and was not happy.

"Keep your eyes and mouth open," said the soldier with

the tanks on his back, "this stuff tastes bad and stings a little, but is harmless."

A white cloud engulfed Baron.

The soldier kept the spray going until he heard Baron coughing. "Now, that wasn't so bad."

Baron's eyes were pink and he was still choking on the gas, but he figured it would have been much worse if he had not been wearing the ectoskin. He had seen others double over and hit the ground puking up their guts. And he could still see, blurry, but he wasn't two-fisting his eyeballs out of their sockets. *This damn ectoskin is probably covered in coronavirus. If I get out of this alive, I am going to track down that snake oil salesman, Vincent, and break my size elevens off in his ass.*

The flamethrower soldier pulled out a black fabric circle and laid it on the ground. "Step backwards one step."

Baron did and felt the thick rubber soles beneath his feet.

"Put your hands at your sides and don't move."

He obeyed.

The soldier pressed a button on his wrist-mounted controls and the black fabric circle inflated around Baron's body then collapsed, mummifying him. "Do not try to walk. We will transport you from here."

Baron couldn't see through the black fabric but felt a cold gentle breeze blowing up his face; recycled air, he assumed. He was rocked slightly forward and then tilted back. A strap tightened across his chest. He began to move. *How humiliating, being wheeled away on a hand truck like a piece of luggage. I'm going to kill Vincent.*

Baron could not imagine how long he had been travelling, or where he was being taken. He knew when the hand truck stopped moving, he was probably in a military vehicle.

Without sight, or sound, or any tactile sensation, time became meaningless. It wasn't until he felt himself being tilted backward and hand-trucked away that time restarted. Beads of sweat ran down his face. A peppermint tanginess creeped into the corners of his mouth and stung his eyes. Then the bright glare of the facemask caused him to squint as he peered around the sterile white room. Cold air forced its way into his nostrils with the burning vengeance of too much cinnamon. Unable to move his arms or legs he must still be strapped to the hand truck.

The wall parted slightly before him and in walked a person of undistinguishable description in a white hazmat suit. The room was bigger than he could determine because it took several steps before the person was close enough for him to see a woman's face in the mask.

He asked, "where am I?"

"Chicago, Illinois Department of Public Health, The Coronavirus Assessment Division," the woman answered politely but curtly. "And before you ask, why am I here, let me start with why you are here. You tried to cross into the Yellow Zone of Fort Wayne, Indiana, with active Covid-19 variants in your system. That's a Class A federal felony." She let the words linger for a moment and as he was about to object, she continued, "and it does not matter whether you knowingly tried to cross state lines with the virus or did not know you are infected, the law remains the same."

"I don't have Covid-19," Baron quickly objected. He knew a Class A felony carried a death sentence, and while you could be a convicted murderer and get twenty-five years, a virus carrier always got death. "I had it years ago in the initial breakout and have since been clean."

"Mr. Dreiser, our records do not show you having Covid-19 before or being treated at any government-approved facilities." She picked up a clipboard from a desk that was below his eyesight. She flipped back and forth between pages. "It says here you denied your identity at the time of your arrest?"

"No! Not my identity, my positive test."

"Please, confirm your identity for me, Mr. Dreiser."

Baron tried to keep his poker face on. He could see the papers in the reflection of her facemask. He quickly scanned for pertinent information. "My name is Donald Dreiser. D.R.E.I.S.E.R, some pronounce it Dr8Sir, but it is actually, Drys Err. I was born June 22, 1987, and I'll be forty-two on my birth-day. Do you need my address in Lima?"

"No, that won't be necessary. I am Ms. Delta Grant, the medical administrator of this facility," the woman returned the clipboard out of sight. "As you probably know, mental confusion is one of the signs of Covid infection. But the only way to be sure if you are infected and with what variant is a blood test. Do you consent?"

"Do I consent?"

"Of course," Ms. Grant smiled a practiced and facetious smile, "this is still America. You are within your rights to deny permission to me for collecting a sample for testing." She held up a hand to stop him from answering too soon. "But if you do not want to give a sample, then we will have to hold you in a quarantine center for up to thirty days observation. Let me warn you, after thirty days in one of those facilities, you will have Covid and probably leave through the crematorium. However, if you volunteer a blood sample, you will be held here for about three days while the lab tests are run, in a private room. And if they come back clean, you will be sent on your way."

"And if the test comes back… less than we hope?"

"You will be admitted into the hospital for treatment," Ms. Grant maintained her smile, "we have an excellent record for treating most of the variants."

"Ok, test away," Baron said, "I'd stick out my arm, but I can't move it."

"Of course not. You are still in the antiviral wrap. You will be taken to your isolation cell… room. You will be sanitized and then a blood sample taken. Do I have your consent?"

"Yes." Baron tilted backward and was on the move again. "Hey! Have you been there the whole time? HEY! I'm talking to you." He realized there was no one to answer him as he passed through a slit in the side of the room and into a darkened, mirrored tunnel. He was on a conveyor belt passing through various stages of decontamination sprays and colored lights. The wrap dissolved and his clothes were drenched in one fluid then another. A voice warned him to close his eyes and open his mouth, then a bluish cloud appeared before him. He came out of the cloud in a six-by-eight-by-ten-foot-high cell with stainless steel fixtures and a vinyl covered cot. "An isolation room my ass!" he shouted to no one.

The front wall of the cell turned clear. A red-haired woman with bright golden eyes set deep in a line-riddled face stood with a large Afro-American man to her left and a young, slim woman with black curly hair to her right. "It's still better than the quarantine facilities. There, you would be in a dorm with maybe fifty others."

"Ms. Grant, I presume."

"Correct," she stepped forward and motioned the large man to follow her. He did, pushing a small cart with a black box to the clear wall. A round, red outline appeared on the wall where the box made contact. "Please pull up your left sleeve and stick your arm through the hole where you see the red lights."

"What is this? Some kind of magic, or a Trekkie gizmo?" Baron remained steadfast and far from the glowing wall.

"Without getting super technical, the wall is made from highly charged metallic particles in a constant state of flux. We control the opacity, density, and the electricity flowing through it at all times. Nothing can escape that cell, not even microbes. Nothing can get in either. And just to ease your mind, the air in your cell is recirculated through a closed-circuit grid that heats it to three thousand degrees and then cools it back down to a comfortable seventy-two. Now, stick your arm through the circle so we can draw blood."

Baron pulled up his sleeve, revealing a wristwatch.

"Wait," Ms. Grant commanded. "We have to take your watch. No electronic devices allowed within this facility. You will have to take it off and toss it into the circle."

"What, this old thing?" Baron looked at his arm then back to Ms. Grant. She was not happy. "This is an old Timex. It is completely mechanical. It was my father's."

"I don't care. Hand it over!"

"It's not that I don't trust you," Baron said with a slight smile, "but I don't. This watch means too much to me to just hand it over. You can just send me and my watch to the quarantine center. I'll take my chances there."

"Just give us the watch," said the young woman. Grant snapped an angry look at her, but she continued, "it's not even working. The hands are not moving."

"That's because it needs to be wound. I'm sure you've never seen a watch that is just a watch. It doesn't talk to me, show videos, tell me where I am, or anything else for that matter. It just tells time."

"Put it inside the box. If it is a mechanical device, just a watch, we'll give it right back," Grant said, "you don't want to go to quarantine over something so idiotic as this. Besides, they will confiscate it at the center too."

Baron unsnapped the metal band and carefully placed the watch into the dark hole beyond the red circle of lights on the wall.

The man behind the box twitched, frowned, and pointed to something only they could see from their side. Grant nodded.

"Go ahead and take your watch, it checks out." She waited for him to retrieve the watch and before he put it back on said, "now, stick your arm all the way into the box and don't move."

Baron put his arm through the red circle, and it disappeared into the darkness. A strange sensation ran up his arm and throughout his skin, like a hoard of fire ants attacking him, biting every inch of his body. Then it stopped.

"You can remove your arm now," Grant said, staring at him.

He did and the large black man rolled the box back from the wall. The red circle disappeared and for a second the wall appeared to be solid metal again. Grant was talking to her two workers when the wall cleared again.

"Ok, Mr. Dreiser, that went well. Please do not touch the walls as we charge them from time to time to kill viruses. There is a television above me in the corner," her finger went up and his eyes followed to a section of the wall that was now a screen. "The remote is in the drawer under the bed. Miss Keller will be back in a few minutes with lunch. She is your medical aide, anything you need, press the call button on the remote for her." The wall went back to its steel look except for the rectangular television screen in the upper right corner.

How the hell did I let Vincent talk me into this? And why did he double-cross me? It had to be him, I passed two state lines with no problems. Then, BAM. As I get to where HE sent me, I get nicked. Now, they've got my blood, and when the DNA test shows I'm not who I said I was, twenty-five years in prison at the very least.

Baron's internal monologue was interrupted by the curly, black-haired girl with amazing green eyes appearing outside his cell. He jumped off the cot, bolted to the wall, and flung both hands against the barrier. The shock threw him to the floor.

"Hey! Don't touch the wall!" She pushed the cart with the black box up to the wall. "Especially when it's in its clear state. I brought you lunch."

"Thanks," Baron said, picking himself up off the floor. The red circle formed in front of the black box, and he reached inside and pulled out a tray of food and a juice box. He lifted the cover slightly to see a thick sandwich and fries. *Prison food hasn't changed at all.* "You can go. You don't have to watch me eat. I promise I won't try to drown myself with the apple juice."

"I do have to wait," she replied, "I have to retrieve the tray when you are finished. Sorry, can't leave anything behind."

"Of course not," Baron said as he walked back to his cot. Slily, he rolled the ectoskin up his chin, past his mouth, "after all, you know I can take this plastic tray and dig my way out of here. Or perhaps, I'll use it to block the cameras, wherever they are hidden, and signal my Delta Strike Team to come rescue me."

"You wouldn't be the first to try." She smiled.

"You know, you are quite stunning. What's your name?"

"Misty Keller."

"I've never seen a woman with your… features. That tan is more than the coming of summer here in Chicago. Where are you from?"

"Chicago. But I get my looks from an unfortunate pairing of a German father and a Puerto Rican mother."

"Unfortunate? Not in the least," Baron crossed his legs and balanced the tray in his lap to hide his growing interest in his jailer. "If you are the last person I am to see in this world, I consider myself very lucky."

"Are you trying to seduce me into breaking you out?"

"Is it working?"

"Not at all," she laughed. "Hey, eat your fries before they get cold. They are barely palatable hot."

Baron picked up one long fry and was about to swipe it through the ketchup underneath it. He looked at the plate and shoved the potato stick in his mouth. Then he ate another, and then three more at once. He could now make out the red writing hidden beneath the pile of potatoes. He looked at her and she smiled. He swiped the ketchup with two more fries, cognizant of the cameras and microphones planted in his cell.

He quickly finished the fries and half ate the sandwich of thick unknown meat and government cheese. He gulped down the apple juice that was more water than juice and walked back to the place where the red circle had been with the tray.

"All done," he said with a smile. "I guess I was really hungry. Now, about breaking me out of here, Misty."

She did something behind the black box and the red circle appeared. "If you can fit through the circle then you can be a free man."

Baron looked over the circle as if he was sizing it up, then slid the tray through, "maybe when you bring dinner. I hope the hole will be large then. I intend to work up quite an appetite thinking about you."

"I hope not," she laughed the same enchanting way, "no one wants to see that."

"Then tell the big guy not to look."

The red circle disappeared. She pulled the cart away from the wall and it turned to steel again.

Baron shouted, "Hey, what did the Red Queen say to you before, just before the wall cleared?" He didn't know if she could hear him or knew what he was talking about.

The wall cleared. "She said, 'Don't get too friendly. He'll probably be dead and in the crematorium in a week.' I hope not, for your sake." The wall steeled up again.

Baron got dinner from Misty, no secret message. A little light flirting, mostly on his part. Then he watched the television screen, two old movies, until the lights went out. Then he lay on his back staring up at the ceiling, waiting.

Misty appeared at the wall. This time, just from her shoulders up was visible, the rest of the wall was steel. "Don't talk, just listen. And stay on the bed. I don't have much time."

Baron leaped to his feet and was inches from her face, "are you Veritas?"

"Didn't I just say, don't talk, just listen?" her face showed her displeasure. "No, I am not Veritas. I work for Vincent."

"That rat bastard. He's the reason I'm in here."

"Look, I have about five minutes before the system backups are finished and the security comes back online. Shut up and get on the cot. You needed to get in here and this was the easiest way. The message is being sent from the computer system on the eighth floor. It's a different system than what runs this place. As far as I know, only Delta Grant has access to that floor. The elevators only go to the sixth floor but there is one staircase past security that goes to the seventh. I believe there is an elevator that goes from the seventh to the eighth floor. In two days, there is a change of the security shift. They work two months on and one off. There is always a lot of chit-chatting going on at the switch. The new team won't know to check your cell, which will give you time to get to the eighth floor and find out what is going on."

"How am I supposed to do that? And there is the little problem that in two days my blood test will reveal who I really am. Then I get shoved into the oven for sure."

"Don't worry, Vincent took care of it. He designed the security software for this place. And he has secured your blood test. It will get swapped out with Don's. He never had Covid. In three days, you'll walk out of here a free man," her voice did not convey her confidence.

"Ok, I guess Vincent is pulling the strings in the cyberworld. But how am I supposed to find my way to the eighth floor?"

"Keep watching TV," she smiled, "you'll see. I got to go."

～

Baron did as he was instructed, he watched TV. Behind a movie or a show, displayed schematics, floor plans, and codes to open the door that he entered the cell appeared. Misty was right, there was only one way to reach the top floor. But that elevator did not just go from the seventh floor to the eighth, it also went all the way to the basement, and three levels below that.

She brought him his breakfast the day of the shift change. She looked worried. There was no playful banter between them. She waited in silence while he hurried through his meal. He returned the tray, and she left.

The encounter or lack thereof left him apprehensive. *Maybe they are onto her. I wonder if they have found out about the messages being broadcasted through the television. Maybe I should abandon this whole idea and just book out of here tonight.*

With nothing else to do, he pressed the remote button and turned on the television, Die Hard, for the third time. Baron was expecting to see the building's layout displayed as a virtual walk-through again. Instead, he read an ominous message in bold capital letters, 'DONALD DREISER WAS KILLED IN AN EXPLOSION WHILE MAKING GASOHOL. MAY HAVE BEEN AN ACCIDENT, BUT A BLOOD TEST WAS UNABLE TO BE OBTAINED. V'

Well, that explains Misty's mood this morning.

A lot of people were making their own synthetic gasoline since the government put restrictions on the amount one could buy. If you wanted to make a run from a zone, gas-powered cars were the only options. EV's could be shut down or run out of power on the road. The movie continued and the walkthrough behind it. Halfway through, he saw another virtual display; an access tunnel that ran under the building. It was an old sewer line that ran from the middle of Chicago to Lake Michigan, an escape route. Baron felt a little better about going through with the plan.

Misty returned with lunch and a smile. They traded innuendoes and she seemed ok. Then Baron noticed while she was talking about his trip to start a new job working for Indiana Transportation, that she was tapping the back of her hand. Just a couple of times at first, but when she knew she had his attention, fingers drummed furiously.

She was sending him a message in Morse Code. 'The Autodriver will be waiting at the escape point. I will bring you the little zapper at dinner, make sure it stays off and hidden.'

'Come with.' He tapped his message with his foot.

'Can't.'

'Can't stay here. They'll know.'

'Think about it. Be ready.'

At dinner, she delivered the zapper as promised. He received a large shock when he pulled the tray through the red circle. This time, his knees buckled, and he fought not to cry out in pain. The zapper was buried in a pile of mash potatoes. He grabbed the gun and a handful of mashed potatoes and shoved it down his pants. "You want a little dessert?"

"Is that supposed to turn me on?" she scoffed.

"Come on," he turned serious, "let me take you away from all of this."

"On an electrician's salary?"

"Is there a problem down there?" Delta Grant voice boomed in the room.

"No, ma'am. I am sure he is just kidding around," Misty quickly replied.

"Mr. Dreiser, mental instability is another symptom of the Gamma variant," Grant's voice was stern.

"Duly noted," Baron walked to his cot, "I'll try to keep the crazy down." He finished eating quickly and in silence. Slid the tray back through the hole and watched as Misty walked away before the wall returned.

Delta Grant was waiting outside the anterior room to the cell chambers. She surprised Misty as she exited the cell block, "what was that?"

"What?"

"Don't play dumb with me," she accused the young woman, "there was a power surge in the portal creator. It looks like it almost killed him."

"You can check the equipment for yourself," Misty spun the cart around, so the display screen faced the older woman. "See, there's nothing there. And I didn't notice anything unusual."

Delta Grant had spent years in the CIA, and she knew a lie when she heard and saw one, "you are done for the night. Clock out. Go home."

"But I have two more hours on my shift," Misty's voice quivered.

"You are relieved."

Misty left the portal generator and started down the corridor towards the elevator. She fought the urge to look back. She hoped Grant had not ordered a search of the cell. They needed just one night.

Delta entered the cell block and stood watching Baron. From her side, the wall was clear glass as always. She saw the stainless-steel barrier keeping him prisoner. Sitting on his cot, he was staring directly back at her.

From the first time he had shuddered reaching into the

box she knew something was not right with him. Every time he reached in his appearance flickered momentarily. His hair flashed from dark brown to black. His facial features shifted slightly, nose and eyes moved on their own. Sometimes, his skin tone faded or darkened for a second. Delta did not believe he was who he said he was, not from the moment she met him.

The television screen lit up with a single word, "GO."

Baron jumped off the cot and started tapping the wall in the corner of the cell. Two taps above his head, three about chest height, and a single tap on either side of that. A door appeared in the wall, slid backward, then sideways. The long black corridor looked dangerous in its emptiness but there was no turning back. He hoped the guards were preoccupied as planned and the cameras frozen with an image of himself on the cot.

He followed the corridor until he came to ladder rungs on the wall. He started climbing. According to the building blue-prints, he was on the third floor in the utility access tunnel. He climbed to the top, the sixth floor. The building was separated at that level. He opened a door and was in the server room. A room that was always unmanned. At the end of the room was a door and beyond it, a short hallway to the only stairs to the seventh floor.

Baron pulled the little zapper out of his pants and switched it to stun. *Please, God, don't let there be anyone in the hallway now.* He cracked the door back and peeked around the opening. His prayers were answered; the way was clear. He ran a few feet to the next door and disappeared into the stairwell. He froze in front of the black globe of the security camera mounted on the ceiling. He imagined sirens going off and flashing lights giving away his position.

Snap out of it and move your ass. He took the stairs two at a time. At the top he ripped the door open and spun into the corridor ready to fire. The place was deserted. The elevator was a mere ten feet ahead. He got to the panel and punched in, "666." Vincent's idea of a joke. *If there's an army on this elevator when it opens, I'll tell them, the devil made me do it.*

The elevator arrived empty. This was starting to look like a cake walk to Baron. He was going to have to take back all those evil thoughts he had about Vincent. The elevator had two buttons, an up arrow and a down arrow. He pushed the up arrow.

The ride was short, naturally; the doors opened to a small vestibule and beyond that was another computer room. There were a dozen desks with monitors and keyboards. Baron sat at the first one and took off his watch. He wound it up and then typed in, "666," on the keyboard. The monitor came to life. It displayed a list of names, addresses, and dates. All women, hundreds of them, in a column, the date they died. There were columns of other information he couldn't decipher. Baron wasn't sure what it meant but he pulled the stem out from his watch and started recording the screen as the names scrolled by.

His watch was mechanical, but the crystal was made of millions of microdots. He could record a vast number of images when the gears were turning. Each tick of the second hand recorded another image on the crystal. He glanced up and saw a light at the far end of the room, another area beyond the computer room. He stopped the watch from recording and strapped it back on his wrist. He was sure he had gotten enough of the information Vincent had sent him for. He went to the door and cautiously peeked through the vertical slit of a window. Then the door slid open.

Well, this is what you came to see.

He psyched himself up to step into the room. It was voluminous. Six rows of what looked like coffins stretched far down the floor. He couldn't count the number, maybe a hundred, maybe two. This had to be the morgue. *Strange. Covid cases are all incinerated. Why would they need a morgue?* He approached the first one and recoiled.

There was a body inside, alright, but she was alive. Hooked up to an oxygen mask and tubes. And she was pregnant. Very pregnant. He looked in the next one and the one after that, all had pregnant women on what he believed was life support. The names on the computer screen started making sense, somewhat. He walked down the row past the baby farm to another door.

It led to a much smaller room. Fewer coffins, much smaller too, lined up in neat rows. As he passed between them a wave of sadness overtook him, they were empty. He reached the end and found a few, ten to be exact, had infants in them. They looked premature.

"Hard to look at, isn't it?"

Baron spun around.

Delta Grant was standing at the other end of the room.

Has she been following me the whole time? Did she send out the missive that brought me here? Or did my luck just run out? "Veritas?"

"What?" She was caught off guard by the question, "Oh no, you found me out." She laughed. "No, Mr. Baron Beard, I am not your elusive leaker of classified information." She crossed the room towards him, ignoring the zapper he clutched tightly in his hand. "But I do know who you are now. And please don't think that little taser gun is going to get you out of here. I'm wearing shielded armor under my clothes."

"I'll hold onto it just in case." Baron pointed the gun at her head before she got within arm's reach. "Let me guess. You are running your own little genetic lab up here, and things are not going well. Answer me this, if you will, is this a private operation or are you on the government dime here?"

"Does it matter," she replied coldly, "the only thing that matters are results. The only way out of this hell we are in is to have someone born with antibodies that we can replicate into a working vaccine.”

"And all those women out there, are good Americans, volunteers for the cause.”

"It would be beautiful if that was true,” she sidestepped towards another door. "But it's hard to ask people to volunteer to be infected with a deadly disease. Some of these women come to us from red zones already infected with the virus and we impregnate them. Some come clean and pregnant, and we infect them. And then there is the third group, neither pregnant nor infected and we get them both.” Delta swung open the side door letting the hum of the incinerator fill the room. "Unfortunately, most of the women do not live long enough to give birth. And so far, the few babies that were born don't have the necessary antibodies or survive to develop them. But we keep trying.”

Baron surmised the incinerator was too small for the mothers. It was for the infants. Delta had shown it to distract him. He was not going to let her get the upper hand. He flipped the switch on the gun to the deadly setting and extended it at her forehead, "you're a monster. You are going to pay for what you are doing to these women and children.”

"Hahaha, I'm not the monster, Covid is. The Gamma variant is Godzilla and King Kong rolled into one. It's easily transmissible and one hundred percent fatal. Mr. Beard, in five to ten years, we… the human race will be at extinction levels. If we don't find a cure or vaccine to stop the spread soon… it's game over.” Delta closed the door but remained where she was. "You think I'm the only one doing this? Think again! There are labs like this in every country around the world. And in some countries—I think you can guess which ones—are taking, let's call it a proactive approach. There are places where if one person dies from this variant, they burn the whole town to the ground, houses, people, pets, everything. Without warning.” She stood cold and impassionate. "I have the pictures in my office if you want to see them. Have you asked yourself this, why are you here?"

"I know why I'm here." Baron pushed back his disgust. He had to stay focused. He had to make it out of here alive. "Veritas sent that message to uncover your dirty little secret. I am sure if you asked, some people would come forward. They always do."

"My God! You are naïve. The people who jumped out of airplanes over Europe or stormed the beaches of France to save the world from tyranny are dead. Today, we have people whose first concern is, 'What's in it for me?'" She shook her head in disappointment. "We have people now, who shoot a store clerk dead rather than put on a simple mask to save her life. That is why we had to enact stricter laws, not to take away personal freedom, but to protect the greater population from themselves. And then there are those like you, gullible. You're a corporate spy." She stepped forward as his gun dropped a bit lower. "There is no Veritas. She is a conglomerate of government and corporation leaks designed to manipulate and fool the people.

"Your friend, Vincent Meyer—we know all about him— sent you here to steal our research. The country or person who develops a weapon against this virus holds the power. I am sure he would like it to be him. As would dozens of others. You asked if I work for a private company or the government, I am the Director of Homeland Security. Now, if you give me the taser and your watch. I know you recorded data with it, I will walk you out of here. It is the only way you get out of here alive."

"I'm not that naïve." Baron quickly weighed his options, "What is to stop you from shooting me in the back?"

"What's the point in doing that?" she reasoned. "Without the data to back up your story, you go from journalist to conspiracy nutjob. Killing you will only throw more fuel on an already out of control dumpster fire. Your friend is smart. But that is the trouble with geniuses, they are too smart to see the obvious flaws in their plans. He sent you in here wearing an ectoskin. If I may," she reached into her lab coat pocket slowly retrieving a makeup compact mirror and popped it open. "He probably told you the ectoskin was some kind of antiviral suit. It was really to mask your true identity, meet Mr. Dreiser."

Baron saw a reflection, but it wasn't his. The person in the mirror had brown hair, light brown eyes, and was very Caucasian. He had been lied to, from beginning to end. He was speechless.

Delta saw the shock sink in. She was used to the reactions of people when their world collapsed around them. They reacted in one of two ways, complete surrender, or irrational violent outburst. And she knew there was no way of foretelling which way each person would turn.

"As I said, Vincent outsmarted himself. There is no record of you being here, so, you will have no backup to your story should you go public. But if you walk out of here with me, tell Vincent the eighth floor is a room full of computers, which he already knows, then no harm no foul." She watched for a semblance of resignation in his demeanor. "Or you can try to go out, the only door from this place, into the corridor where a dozen heavily armed soldiers are waiting for you. And if you somehow make it past them, there are forty more on the floor below, and more in the subbasement. All of them with orders to shoot to kill."

Baron wanted the story; he did not want to be the story. He did not trust Grant, but he definitely wasn't going to die for Vincent Meyer's whatever this was. He handed the zapper to her and took off the watch. "This is just a watch, no spy tech or anything like that, I hope you will send it back to me in one piece when you're done."

"If it checks out, I will see to it that you get it back." She tapped a spot under her right ear and said, "we are coming out. Stand at the ready." Delta put the devices in her lab coat pocket and took his arm. They started back through the rooms of coffin-like medical units. "We are not the bad guys here and if we had the time to wait for nature to deliver the antibodies, we would. We simply don't have the time. We are very close to the end of our rope. Then, the nuclear option is our only recourse. You get that, right?"

Baron did not respond as the last door opened, and he was face to face with three teams of four M16s toting soldiers in black armored gear ready to annihilate him. The elevator opened and four more heavily outfitted soldiers awaited him. He grabbed her hand as she was about to pass him to the guards.

She understood his apprehension and got in the elevator too.

The elevator doors opened in the dimly lit subbasement parking garage thirty-six feet below Chicago. Delta pushed Baron from the elevator cab as the four soldiers filed out.

She remained within the elevator, "alright, men, you can handle it from here. You know what to do with him."

The lead soldier stumbled over a black-outfitted soldier lying on the ground. He looked around at the dozens of soldiers in their battle gear strewn about the garage. He snapped his rifle up to his shoulder preparing to fire.

Baron's eyes were blinded by the onslaught of floodlights ahead of him. He turned to the side, trying to save his sight. The soldiers' visors turned black, to protect their eyes. They were spreading out, moving away from him in an automatic defensive maneuver learned over years of practice. He saw them drop in rapid succession before they could fire a shot.

He flung himself back into the elevator and threw a perfect shoulder tackle into Delta's midsection. She hit the back wall of the cab and fell face first on the floor in front of him.

High School State Champion Defensive Back two years in a row. I still got the moves. He fished in her pockets for his watch and zapper.

The parking garage returned to its dismal visibility.

Misty called out, "leave her! We got to get out of here before more troopers are called in."

"I need my watch," Baron yelled back.

"It can't be that important to you to die for."

"It has the information I came here for," he flipped Delta over and pulled the items from her other pocket. "Got it!" He held the watch up triumphantly.

"Wonderful, let's go."

Baron ran to the SUV jumping over two soldiers as he did. He dove through the side door and landed in Misty's lap. "I'm glad you decided to come with. You did all this? You're bad ass."

"It was nothing," Misty said pushing him off her. "I set the rifle on wide disbursement. It knocked them all out at once. The real trick was getting the other four without hitting you. Lucky for you, they made it easy."

Rattling noises came from the rear of the SUV as it raced through the old pitch-black sewer tunnels of Chicago.

"Don't tell me, we are being shot at," Baron said.

"I told you the army wouldn't be far behind. I had to crash through two gates to get to you."

"I hope Vincent popped for the bulletproof paint job."

"So far, it appears he has."

"Obstruction ahead," a female robotic voice informed them.

"That is so sexist."

"Forget about that!" Baron jumped to the front of the vehicle's cabin. "How far ahead? Hit the lights!"

"Five hundred feet," the SUV complied, and the head-lights revealed a solid brick wall they were barreling towards.

The shooting stopped. The two armored vehicles blocked the tunnel behind them.

Baron asked the AI, "what's beyond the wall?"

"Lake Michigan."

"Give me that rifle," he commanded Misty as he popped open the Moonroof.

"Are you going to fire on those Humvees? They are equipped with antitank rounds now."

"No." He said as he flipped the switch on the rifle to high power. He blasted the brick wall, dropped back down inside the SUV, and the Moonroof slammed shut. The explosion sent brick particles in every direction and especially back at their vehicle. They were within fifty feet of the wall and long jagged cracks ripped through the bricks ahead of them. "I hope that was enough. Get ready to go for a swim."

The wall exploded and a violent white fist punched the SUV, throwing it back up the tunnel. It slammed into the two Humvees and landed on its wheels. The tunnel filled with water quickly. The Humvees engines stalled, and its occupants abandoned their pursuit in their scuba gear. They were prepared for all circumstances, but flow of the lake proved to be too much for them to fight.

Slowly, the SUV fought its way through the flooded tunnel to the hole in the wall and into the Great Lake beyond. Once in the water, paddles unfolded from the tires' rubber threads and the SUV proceeded effortlessly as it was designed to do.

"Did you know this SUV was equipped for underwater operations?" asked Misty.

"I had no clue what I just did wasn't going to kill us. It was our only option, so I rolled the bones."

"Where to now, captain Ahab?"

"Canada. I'll write the story and put it on the internet

from there. I can never go home, but I am sure Vincent will find a way to get you back in the States."

"Actually, I'm not from the United States. But I am sure Vincent will help me get back home."

❧

04 July 2033. THE TRUTH BE TOLD. *vincit omnia veritas* (truth conquers all things).

The world's death toll still climbs. Unconfirmed totals have sixty percent of all humans, over five billion, have died of the virus or at the hands of their governments. Towns and cities are firebombed every day. Humanity is reaching extinction levels.

A secret laboratory in the United States of America has developed a vaccine from a group of children born with natural immunities. They are inoculating certain members of their population for world control in the post pandemic world.

The five-nation super pack of China, France, Great Britain, Iran, and Russia demands the US release the vaccine or face nuclear war. The United States denies any breakthrough in the fight against COVID-19 and the Gamma variant.

Baron Beard, living in an undisclosed location in the Northwest territory, has yet to write his story.

THE END

THE MOTH

Part 1

Calliope awoke earlier than usual that day and quietly washed and dressed in her room. She wore her favorite white frock over her royal-blue flair dress. She had on her white sneakers which looked red from the dirt of the vineyards. The morning sun caused the deep red grapes to shine like blood drops on the green vines outside her window.

She peeked out of her bedroom door. The hall was empty. Her brothers' doors were open and large white squares painted the dark stone floor. Her father's door at the end of the hall was closed. She heard him come in late last night, the usual drunken voices of a village woman, and his vulgarity. *Good thing,* she thought, *She probably left with all his money hours ago. And he's still deep in a stupor.*

Today was August 29, 1994, her eighteenth birthday. She would make it down the backstairs, through the kitchen, out the pantry door, and Jacques would be waiting for her in the village square. She'd climb on the back of his motorbike, wrap her arms around his waist, and he would take her far, far away from the House of Rancid Grapes.

That was her plan. But when she reached the kitchen all her plans vanished. Ameri DeNoirre was sitting at the old wooden table, a bottle of wine and two glasses on it. His glass was perpetually empty, no matter how many times he filled it. The other sat full and untouched before a man with gray and black hair and dead cold eyes.

"You are eighteen today," Ameri slurred.

Calliope was surprised he remembered. He hadn't for years. "Yes. I am going to the market. We have no milk or eggs for breakfast."

The stranger smiled. His lips barely parted, "So, she can cook too?"

Calliope shot an angry glare at him. An instant hatred gripped her. What business was it of his, whether she could cook or not.

"And such a fire she has," the stranger laughed at her. "Yes, she will do. You are quite right, she is worth every franc."

"Then, it is settled," Ameri stated.

"What is settled? What will I do?" Demanded Calliope.

"Contessa Calliope DeNoirre, let me introduce you to your husband, Mienheart Eldersteen," her father badly butchered the stranger's name, "as soon as the bank opens."

"Mienhard Eldinstein," the stranger fixed it with a regal German accent, "at your pleasure."

Calliope's mind went numb, as if all the air had been sucked out of the room. She tried to speak but there was no sound in the void. Her father, this man, their faces twisting with horrific grins. She grabbed the back of a chair, steadied herself. Surely, she was still in her bed. This was a nightmare.

"You will have your money," the German said, shattering the trance she was under. "Two hundred thousand, as agreed!"

"What do you two think you are doing," she screamed to

be sure she was really awake. "You cannot sell me like I am the family cow."

"Calliope, the harvest has been a dismal failure this year. The worst one yet. Surely, you know this—"

"I don't care," Calliope was reaching breaking point. "I am leaving. Today! Now! I am going to meet Jacques and we are never coming back!"

"Ah, the boyfriend you mentioned," the German said coldly. "In ten minutes, the police will arrive at his house. They will find a package. It contains a large amount of heroine. Your Jacques will be in prison until he is older than I."

"Unless, I agree," she muttered.

"Yes," he said.

Calliope knew Jacques' life was over.

"He didn't spoil you, did he? Ameri, I told you, I will not pay for damaged goods."

"Yes. Yes, we made love many times," Calliope desperately blurted out. "In fact, I carry his baby. That is why I must leave today," she added.

"She lies," Ameri laughed. "She has barely kissed the boy. The doctor will be here to confirm this."

Calliope could take no more degradation. She fainted. When she came to the doctor had finished his examination. She didn't feel like herself. She didn't feel like anyone. She awoke dead, inside and out.

"Contessa," her father put his arm around her shoulder as if to comfort her. "These things happen all the time. You are saving the family's vineyard from ruin. It's your duty. Your boy, he will not go to prison. And I found a man who is advanced in years. He will be dead while you are in the prime of your life. And you will have all his money."

Although Calliope heard his words they did not register. The whole vile affair was a never-ending nightmare. The wedding, her first and only night in his bed, his stubby fingers grabbing and pawing her flesh. His weight pinning her down. His legs forcing hers apart until he could push his thick hard flesh into her, seeking the fire he saw in her father's kitchen. There was none.

"Our network went down at midnight, Mr. Rankin. It was down for more than 15 minutes. During that time every student's grade was changed to A's. Mr. Rankin, this could jeopardize everyone's graduation." The priest leaned forward across the desk. He took the young man's cheeks in hand and squeezed painfully. "Except for the backups, Mr. Rankin. You forgot about the backups. We restored everyone's grades to what they were before the finals. Teachers will be working all weekend calculating grades for those who are borderline. I have one question for you, Mr. Rankin. Why? You have straight A's. You would have graduated."

The words, "would have" echoed like a gong in his head. "How do you know it was me," Harry said, shaking loose from the old priest's grip he was sure wanted to break his jaw. "I mean, what makes you think this was my doing. It could have been anyone…"

"You by-passed several security protocols. Rebooted the system each time the password failed. Very clever. No one but you… No one but you… No one but you…"

That was the day he got expelled, it was his birthday, eighteen and no diploma.

"No one but you? No one but you? No one but you?" This time it was the trial judge asking him, no, demanding he give up the names of the others involved before passing sentence. Those words echoed in his head the day he went to prison, July 14, 2007, Bastille Day. Give or take a couple hundred years. Strange, four years of High School French and all he knew was the day they stormed the prison.

"BRRRONK… Brronk… bronk…" The hard sound of the prison alarm ended his dream. But it was more like recollections, rumblings from long ago. It was the last time he'd hear that sound, seven years were done.

The guard came to let him out of his cell first. They escorted him through the corridors to cheers and shouts of, "See you soon, Birdie."

"See you never," he replied good-heartedly. The guards were taking him to the release room. Making sure no one killed him before he was out the gate. Not that Harry had enemies, he didn't, but it was protocol. The last month you are almost in isolation. Some people would want you to serve your entire time and then kill you before you walked out the gate.

"No one came to get you, Harry," said the guard at the outside gate. "You want to wait; I'll call you a cab."

"Mike, what are you doing at the gate?"

"I wanted to be the last person you saw in here, Harry. How about that cab ride?"

"No, thanks, Mike," Harry Rankin smiled, "this is the first time in seven years I can walk more than a hundred feet and not hit a wall. I think I'd rather walk to the train station."

"I hope I never see you again, Harry," the guard said and pressed the green button.

The gate swung open and Harry hurried through it, "If you do, it won't be in here."

He started down the road, the tall gray walls of Sing Sing on his left, and the world ahead of him. He turned down parole twice. He wanted to walk away from this place free and clear. And now he was. The air was cool and crisp on this autumn morn. It smelled so much fresher on this side of the wall. He had $42.37 when he went into prison. He had just over three grand today. Money he made from working and doing favors for other prisoners, much more of it from favors. It was enough to raise the eye of the property clerk. He left with his money and nothing else, he told the guards to let the boys take whatever they wanted from his cell. He doubted they would.

He was a mile down the road when a red corvette convertible hooked a u-turn and roared to a stop just ahead of him. A woman jumped out in a red skirt, cut above the knee, a low-cut black tank top, and black strapped heels. "I'm so sorry I'm late, baby. There was an accident on the highway, and I got stuck in traffic."

"For seven years," spewed Harry.

"Baby, I wanted to come," she pleaded, "but you know Blackie."

"Yeah, I think I do. It was his plan that sent me to prison or was it yours? No matter. I sent letters. I called. Not a fucking word! You can get back in the car, we're done. I'm done!"

Harry stood there on the side of the road, staring at Rachael Dove. She had filled out, grown up since he went to prison. She had been in her teens when he met her, bartending for Samuel Blackwell, Blackie, in one of his clubs in Queens. One hundred and five pounds of trouble, most of it, tits and ass. She had a look that got men thirsty and made her tips. Caramel skin and green eyes like a traffic light that beckoned you onward. And her voice, Sing Sing was probably named for her.

Harry shook off the vision. He snapped back to reality, "you're seven years too late. I don't need the ride anymore."

He walked past the car and didn't look back. It was a long while before the corvette raced past him. Maybe she was sitting there hoping he'd turn back, change his mind. Maybe she was crying uncontrollably and just managed to compose herself enough to drive. He thought he felt a teardrop hit his face as she whizzed by. But that was a fantasy, not a good one, wouldn't do to have the boss' daughter smash up the car because her ex-boyfriend gave her the cold shoulder. Blackie would surely turn him into dog food. The real reason for her delay, she was reporting to her daddy.

~

Harry moved into a nice hotel on 72nd Street. It rented month to month, a kitchen, bath, and bedroom. It wasn't big; maybe quadruple the size of his cell. He paced it off to be sure, but it had walls separating the three rooms. And he could afford it.

The Outside took some getting used to. He didn't think he'd miss the alarms, or the screams. There were street noises that he wasn't used to anymore, traffic, sirens, and gunshots. A week had passed, and he hadn't slept night or day, a couple of hours here and there, but way too many hours lying awake.

Like when he first went in, lying on his back, thinking of her. Shaking from withdrawal and thinking of her.

KNOCK… KNOCK… KNOCK…

Harry walked the seven steps to the door. Who the hell could it be? No one knew he was here.

"It's me."

Words he had heard a million times before. Without a thought he unlocked the door. Rachael leaped into his arms, onto his lips, her tongue burrowing its way back into his heart. Her legs wrapped around his hips; her arms encircled his neck. Harry kicked the door shut and stumbled seven steps back to the bed. Rachael straddled him and pulled her top over her head. She was struggling to get it untangled from her hair. Her breasts bounced and wiggled before him as she did. Big, golden brown, more perfect than he remembered.

He reached out and cupped each dark rippled nipple gently in his fingers. Electricity shot through his body and her top flew across the tiny room. Suddenly, the single bed was much smaller.

He had merely thought of her, and here she was. He felt

weak, confused, maybe he was dreaming, delirious from lack of sleep. She was kryptonite to Superman, heroine to Harry. "Wait… What the hell are you doing here? Did Blackie send you?"

"Yes," she cooed. "Now, shut up," she ordered, "I have seven years to make up for."

He had seven years of anger, disappointment, and hate built-up inside him. She had grown, filled out, and matured. Her arms and hands were strong, and she raked his bare chest. Her legs were curved and shapely, smooth and soft to his touch. He ran his hands up to her hips, they had rounded and firmed up, they pinned him to the bed.

Rachael was all over him. Voraciously kissing and stripping clothes from his body. She pulled the boxers from him with such force his unit painfully slapped his stomach. She gripped him with both hands and gave him a few tugs. She knew he didn't need it; he was as hard as he could be, but it felt good in her hands. She needed it.

She rose up before him like a bronze goddess and engulfed him. Her soft searing body swallowed all of him. Her mouth sucked the sigh from his lips. The fever of her folds intensified as she rode up and down on him.

He grabbed and ripped at her flesh. Squeezing and biting her, digging his nails into her as he slammed into her body. Inflicting pain and eliciting moans of pleasure she muffled with his neck in her teeth. She bathed him in as much ecstasy as the seven years of absence had stored in her. Rachael took all of his pain into herself as if she needed to fill the emptiness she had there. As hard as Rachael rode him, as forcefully as he drove into her, Harry could not reach satisfaction. Hot and exhausted, he abruptly stopped, pushed her against the wall, and went to sleep.

～

Moonlight blinded him. Rachael lay next to him, slowly stroking him. "You can stop that now," he told her.

"It's ok, I like the way you feel," she said and took longer, slower strokes.

"Well, I don't," he snapped. "You got what you came for, go back to your daddy."

Rachael stopped and rolled on top of him. "What I came for is you. And you haven't given me that yet." She giggled like a schoolgirl. Like she used to do when he touched her sweet spot. She was rubbing herself on him and giggling.

"Still ticklish I see. Why don't you stop toying with me and tell me why you're here, Dove?"

"I already told you. I've waited seven years. I've been in prison too. I want you." She pushed her upper body away, which drove her lower half down on him.

He groaned. He called her Dove. He only called her by her last name when he was really mad.

"You can do whatever you want to me, I don't care. Whatever it takes to get you off, I'll do it. You can beat me if you like."

"What? Hell no, Rache!" Harry was pissed. He only called her Rache when he really wanted her. Those green eyes sparkled in the moonlight. "Kryptonite."

"Oh, yes, Superman. I'm yours." She sucked in her breath and held it. Gasping a little each time he pushed deeper into her. He flipped and rolled on top of her for his final penetration. She let out an elongated, "YESSS."

Harry looked her over in the moonlight. She was covered in scratches and bite marks. She would look worse before this night was through. He grabbed her hands and pinned them above her head in his left hand. He slapped her thigh with his right. She spread wider in response. He quickened his pace and gave her full deep strokes. He was working toward an orgasm. Rachael was already having them. Her eyes glowed. Kryptonite.

Rachael felt tiny explosions growing larger inside her. Fire poured into her as his hand locked tighter around her wrist. His muscles were taunt and steeled. He pounded her pelvis with his full weight and then some. Her thighs ached as they were being forced wider, beyond their limit. Her body screamed from the hammer against her velvet walls. Each throbbing spastic strike unloaded enough hot fluid to fill her to bursting. It seemed he would never stop. He couldn't stop. He flooded her body.

Calliope sat at the make-up table picking out a few pieces of jewelry for the trip. Madame Olga was finishing packing the third suitcase of clothing. "I don't know why you bother, Olga. When we get to New York, he will drag me to a dozen boutiques and buy a hundred outfits I shall never wear."

"Yes, of course he will," her handmaiden agreed, "but this time we are going to New York. I have nieces there, one who is about to graduate from high school. I'm sure she would like one of your gowns for prom. If that is alright with you?"

"Yes, that is fine," Calliope smiled, "in fact, give her all of them. She and her girlfriends can have the best dressed prom in New York City."

"Countess, what is taking you so long?" Mienhard bellowed from somewhere below.

Calliope bristled at the name. As she did every time he called her that. She grabbed a handful of jewelry and tossed them in the bag. "Here, pack this and let's go. Don't know why he is in such a hurry, it's not like his jet will leave without him."

"But still, you know how he gets before he travels. You don't want to upset him."

Calliope knew exactly how he got when he was angry. She had learned that lesson a month after entering this marble prison. She had arrived in a floral peasant dress, her father and brothers had thrown all her clothes into a bag and hurried her out the door as soon as the marriage license was signed by the priest.

She thought they were all afraid the police would bust in and lock them all up for white slavery. Oh, if only they had. Instead, when they landed in Greece, Mienhard had his driver take them to every shop in three towns, and bought her every outfit that fit.

And when she wore only one or two of those, he told her she must prefer French designers. Back on the plane to Paris, hours of being dragged around and dressed up like a doll. It was there they met Madame Olga and he persuaded her Calliope needed someone to properly look after her. Olga closed up her shop and flew back to Greece with them. Two years later, Madame Olga told Calliope that she had looked so lost she was afraid for her life, and that was the reason she had taken the job.

It was after Paris that Mienhard Eldinstein threw the first of many parties. He said it was in her honor, but it was for his ego. Madame Olga dressed her in a lace gown with a sheer pale underlining. Calliope hated it, it made her look naked. Of course, Mienhard picked it out. He came in to put the finishing touches on her, diamond and sapphire earrings and a necklace that matched the azure of her eyes. And he topped her off with some silly headpiece crown.

He led her around the room like she was a French poodle at a dog show. Instead of a leash and collar, it was his arm and a weighty diamond bracelet. He introduced her as his wife, the Countess Calliope Eldinstein. She cringed every time. Didn't matter if he said it in French, German, Greek, or English, which he spoke very poorly, the effect on her was the same. Finally, a German woman with giant jiggling juggernauts caught his attention and she slipped free of her leash.

She was going to return to her room and wait out the circus below. Two French men trapped her on the stairs, drunk and full of questions. She answered none of them. Not even, "Ce qui est votre nom," which they kept repeating after every other question.

Before she could escape, Mienhard was there. He made an excuse to take her upstairs. In her room he asked, "Ce qui est votre nom?"

Calliope stood defiant and silent. After a moment, he sent the back of his left hand crashing into her cheek. His knuckles landed hard, and she tasted blood. He asked again in German, "Wie heiBen Sie?"

When she didn't answer he backhanded her again with his right. He asked her again in Greek. She was prepared for another strike when she saw the glee in his eyes. He was enjoying her defiance and her punishment.

"Contessa Calliope DeNoirre," she replied.

He struck again, "Nicht."

"Contessa Calliope Eldinstein."

"Nicht."

"Countess," she choked on the word, "Calliope Eldinstein." Didn't he know they meant the same thing? And from then on, whenever she made him mad, which was as often as she could, he responded with knuckles to her cheek.

Calliope spoke French, German, and English very well. Mienhard spoke German, French, and Greek. Calliope refused to speak any German. She responded to him, however rarely, only in English. No matter how many times he yelled, "In Deutsch," followed by the back of his hand.

Within two months the parties had stopped. Calliope was taking all her meals, breakfast, lunch, and dinner, in her room alone. Mienhard thought it punishment for an unruly child. Calliope found it a welcome relief.

One day, the servants stopped bringing her food. The second day passed and no one came to her room. By the third morning, she was pale and weak as she made her way to the breakfast terrace. Mienhard sat with the big-breasted German woman from the party on his lap feeding him sausages. There was a smaller, less endowed Greek girl next to him. His hand was under the table and probably up her dress from the looks of Madame Olga and the other servants.

Calliope sat across from them. The butler brought a full plate and shamefaced placed it before her. Calliope started eating, not looking up when the trio laughed and made jokes about her in Greek. Mienhard was trying to humiliate her with his noisy, nightly women and his starvation tactics.

Calliope thought him sad and pathetic. His actions had no effect on her because she did not care. But three months had been long enough; she would put an end to this charade and leave this prison. "What do you want from me, you paid $200,000 for my virginity, wasn't that good enough for you?"

"What I paid for was a wife," he replied. The busty woman laughed and Mienhard dumped her on the floor. He ordered them out and the two women ran for the front door.

"Then my father cheated you," she stated. "My father sold you my body that day. But that was all you got, no heart, no soul. Those were not his to sell or something you can buy. Not with money, or dresses, or jewels. So, you might as well let me go back to France and save yourself all this trouble and humiliation."

"Your father is a drunk and a terrible wine maker, but he is a shrewd businessman. If I divorce you for any reason, you get half of everything I own. And upon my death, you get it all."

Calliope unconsciously glanced down at the knife on the table.

"You can't spend it from the gallows, my dear Countess." Mienhard smiled at her like he did in her kitchen.

She picked up the knife and cut a piece of sausage.

"I made a very poor deal that day, my dear Countess, I realize that now. But you are stuck with me."

"But you are not," Calliope pleaded, "you don't have to divorce me. Just let me go, we can get on with our lives."

Mienhard Eldinstein started eating again, he drank some wine.

Calliope hoped he was considering her proposal. After all, what sense did it make to keep her there, she would starve to death before sitting at his table again. He had to know this.

"No. The night in the bar, when your father showed me your picture, I knew I had to have you for my collection. I am an art dealer and collector; look around you, all priceless pieces from all over the world. And you, my dear Countess, are my most treasured possession. I only make love to you once, to perfect you. Make you a woman. You see I have others to perform those duties. You are my wife. You will go where I say go. Wear what I say wear. Do as I say do. No, you can never leave." Mienhard returned to eating. It was final.

Calliope looked at the knife in her hand. She wondered whose heart would be easier to pierce, hers which had already turned to stone. Or his, that is, if he even had one.

From that day forward he dragged her around the world, Madrid, Rome, Paris, London, Cairo, Hong Kong, and now New York. But never to Germany, and it made her wonder.

Harry woke to the smell of bacon and the sight of Rachael at the stove wearing just his shirt. Yesterday, last night, whatever that was, for lack of a better word he called it passion, was gone. This morning, he felt empty.

What was she trying to do, domesticate herself? The small bedroom had two doors; one led to the front door and the other to the kitchen. Why didn't she choose the right door? On the way to the front door, four paces, was the bathroom. She could have showered and been gone. No, she wasn't finished with him yet.

She wanted something more. He rubbed his eyes. He knew what she was here for.

Rachael turned and walked towards the bed with one plate. The plate was piled high with bacon, eggs, and pancakes. Everything was covered in syrup, the way he liked it. He looked past the plate at the one button on his shirt that held it in place. Her neatly trimmed black bush was peek-a-booing through his shirt as she walked.

Don't be a fool, Harry. Kryptonite. Wait for it. He heard the words in his head.

"I hope you're hungry, because I'm starving." She laid the plate on the bed. "Breakfast in bed is a nice way to start the day. And later, we can take a ride out to Queens."

Bam. There it was. "Why would I do that," he said bitterly, "I have no business in Queens."

"Aw, come on, Harry, don't be like that," she fed him a piece of bacon. "You know Blackie sent me to bring you back."

"Ok, then let's go." Harry hopped off the bed and headed for the bathroom.

"You know, he didn't say we had to be there at any particular time," she called out. She heard the shower turn on. She followed the sound to the bathroom. "Oh, so that's where it is. Do you mind?"

Rachael didn't wait for his response. She sat on the toilet, let out a long steady stream, and a satisfied, "Aaahhh. You don't know how long I've been holding that in, Harry… Harry, you don't have any toilet paper!"

"You should have thought about that before you sat down."

"Come on, Harry, don't be cross. Can I get in? You know… rinse off." She said shyly.

"Look under the sink." He commanded.

She saw the roll on the floor and thought twice before using it. She pulled the curtain back. "You know Blackie just wants to do right by you. Step back, I'm gonna flush," she warned.

"And exactly what is do right? What does that mean?" The water got hot but not as hot as he felt now.

"He's going to give you your share from the bank job," Rachael giggled watching him trying to dodge the hot water. "Here, let me get in and do your back for you."

"Rache," damn, did it again, "seven years in prison. I don't really like anybody in the shower with me."

"Oh… Yeah. Sorry, what was I thinking?"

"Hey… Don't worry, nothing like that ever happened," Harry quickly assured her. "So, how much is seven years' worth? And why didn't he just send it with you?"

"I don't know," she said, "me and the guys got a quarter apiece. I'm guessing he'll give you more since you took the rap all by yourself. Blackie is a good guy."

"He's your dad. I'm sure he treats you swell." The sarcasm was like the steam in the air.

"He's the boss; he wants all of his people happy."

Harry stepped out of the shower and grabbed the towel. He left the water running, "Go ahead and get in. I'll bring you a towel."

They ate breakfast. Rachael tidied up, against Harry's wishes. They talked, but not about Blackie, she was out of the bartending business. With two hundred and fifty thousand dollars you don't work for tips anymore. Of course, the money got laundered and came back as a few businesses, one being a boutique that she walked him down to 37th and 7th to show him.

It was a small shop in the heart of the fashion district called, "Lovey Dovey's." Harry burst out laughing. He finally composed himself and said, "You hated me calling you that."

"I know," she was solemn. "But when I got it, that first year, you were all I could think of. I spent so much time crying in here, I nearly drove away all the customers."

They walked around for a while more and then she pulled out her cell phone and summoned a car. Harry didn't recognize the driver, someone new no doubt, but he recognized the look. And the speed in which he showed up, he couldn't have been more than a few blocks away. Probably spent the night parked in front of his building.

Blackie was in the backroom of the bar. The bar was an old Irish pub; it looked the same, still the rattiest place in Astoria. It was where Harry's life took a nosedive, the White Stallion. Two of his friends took him there for some Saturday night fun. Somehow, they ended up in the backroom passing the needle. It was just a one-time high, which turned into a five-year addiction. His two friends dead, the only bright spot in this little corner of hell was a demon he knew as Rachael Dove. She made powerful potions that eased the pain, sometimes slipping him one on the house.

"Hey, pay attention, boy," Blackie barked.

Harry snapped to.

"Here. Before you open the case, let me tell you I appreciate your loyalty. I made sure everyone knew you worked for me." He slid the briefcase across the desk.

Harry opened it and studied the stacks of twenties, fifties, and hundreds. He was speechless.

"It's five hundred thousand dollars."

"Why not a million?" Harry's words dripped sarcasm.

"Expenses, my boy," Blackie replied. "I had to leave a million behind for the dicks to chase down. Then split the five millions with the boys... and girl," he explained glancing at

Rachael. "And, of course, there were the laundry fees. But you got twice what the others got."

Harry closed the case and got up to leave.

"Hold on, Harry," Blackie commanded. "I have a little job for you."

"Really, you just handed me my retirement package."

"I'll double it," Blackie quickly added. "It's a simple task. Right up your alley. Zero risk to you."

"No thanks," Harry turned to the door. "I'll quit while I'm behind."

"Harry, sit down," Blackie said with an unpleasant tone. He slid a photo across the desk to him. "You have to hack her emails. Plant a virus and retrieve some information."

Harry was drawn into the woman's photo, pulled in by her sea-watery eyes. Drowning pools pulling him down and robbing him of air. She was magically crushing him as he peered into her image.

"Harry!" Blackie called him twice before he came out of his trance.

"Humph," Rachael disapproved loudly.

"She… She don't look like, ah, she has anything worth stealing," Harry stumbled over his words and thoughts.

"Not her." Blackie shoved another photo under his nose, "her husband, Mienhard Eldinstein. They are going to be in New York this weekend at a charity event for artists or some bullshit. You are going to make contact with the Countess Eldinstein."

Part 2

Harry was no artist. Luckily, he knew one Jonathan Franklin Kurkman, JFK, a damn good one and pretty successful forger. Until heroin took hold. Harry talked the warden into letting Johnny Boy, what mostly everyone called him, or The President, to teach the inmates art. Painting had a calming effect. Harry ran a class on computer programming. He convinced, conned, the warden into thinking that letting the inmates put their natural talents to good use was more productive and had a better chance to rehabilitate them than putting them to work in the kitchen or laundry.

Johnny Boy taught Harry how to paint a bit and Harry went to work hacking the government systems. But he was calm about it. He started out small, okaying books that could be received by the inmates. Then he moved up to give them more telephone time for a fee. He also arranged for inmates to call banned numbers, giving his "clients" special numbers that automatically rolled over. The President liked that. He returned the favor by painting a portrait of Rachael. In his first two years Harry raved about her, obsessed over her, and went out of his mind because of her. The next two years, Johnny Boy painted the picture when Harry refused to mention her name. He gave it to Harry the day he made parole.

That was a very bad day for Harry. A week later, Harry hacked the state's Justice System and moved his release date forward three years. The next week he put it back. He kept Rachael's picture on his bed propped up against the wall turned backwards. He lined his cell along the floor with the dozen or so pictures Johnny Boy gave him. He was good.

Harry stood outside the three-story brownstone on West 4th Street looking up. The broken, dark diamond-pattern the bricks made, the white marble windowsills that looked like steppingstones to the roof, and the white capitals on each corner pillar that held up the roof, or at least that's what it looked like their purpose was. It was exactly as Johnny Boy had painted it. He had the second floor.

Harry pushed the middle button and waited for an answer. A few minutes later, he pushed again and held it for as long as he had waited. He went through a series of short rapid beeps. Then a woman came on, "Yeah, what'd ya want?"

"Is Jonathan available?"

"I haven't seen him in about two weeks," the speaker crackled. "You con or cop?"

"What?" Harry asked.

"Are you a vick or a dick. Only two types of people come for him, which are you?"

"I'm a friend from upstate, Harry Rankin." He replied, indirectly answering her question.

He saw a hazy figure come down the hall through the frosted glass. She swung open the door; he recognized her instantly, stringy brown-gray hair, long face with sunken cheeks, frail boney body. The President had painted more pictures of her than anything else during his ten-year term. He did a few of her, where she had more color in her cheeks, a sparkle to her eyes, probably a time before they rode the white horse.

"Yeah, it's you," she declared, "you looking for a place to hide from that girl of yours? It's like I said, I haven't seen JFK in weeks, and he owes me three months backs. I'd evict his ass but who'd rent the smelly place now."

"Will this tie him over?" Harry reached into his pocket and pulled out a thick fold of bills.

She snatched the bills like a snake on a mouse. "Maybe, I'll let you know. Go ahead up, the door probably is not locked. Nothing worth stealing."

Nothing worth stealing, Harry thought as he entered and surveyed the apartment, nothing but a man's life's work. In a corner of the kitchen was a 36 by 36 picture of him. The color was all wrong, his face was more reddish than brown, but he got the eyes, nose, and lips right. He turned around and saw a picture of Rachael, she looked perfect. Better than the one he had left in Sing Sing. If he didn't know better, he would have thought she sat for it.

From what he could tell it was only The President and the Landlady in the brownstone. The apartment took up the whole second floor. It wrapped around like a 'L', the kitchen, a right turn then one room after the next. Each littered with paintings, portraits, stills, landscapes, nightmares. He stood in the bedroom staring down. There between the bed and the wall, just outside the bathroom door, lay The President. Hypo hanging from his arm. Harry shook his head and took out his cell phone to call 911.

The apartment filled up quickly and took a long time to empty. The first officer on the scene, a uniform, took out his notebook, "name?"

"Harry Rankin."

"How long have you known the deceased?"

"Four years, we did time together."

"Were you and Mr. Rankin sharing needles?"

"What… NO! You got it…" Before Harry could put together his words the policeman grabbed his left arm and pulled up his sleeve. Seeing no fresh tracks he let go.

"Okay, so what's your name and what's the story with the late Mr. Rankin?"

And just like that, Harry Rankin's life was over. Dead from an overdose, and now he was Jonathan Franklin Kurkman, the artist. He thought about straightening the cop out for a second, but only for a second. He was the one who made the mistake. Jumped to conclusions. Fuck him. "I've been out of town for a while; Harry just got out of the joint. He needed a place to stay. I came home today and there he was, that's the long and short of it."

Harry felt the landlady's eyes on him from the living room. He gave her a look and patted his right hip pocket. He had come for a few paintings; he got a new identity. He had to get to work making sure the records matched up, or he could go back to jail, this time for murder. As soon as the cops left, he headed for a cybercafé. He had left himself plenty of backdoors into the state and fed's computer systems. It was easy enough to swap names on a couple of records. He searched the net and found a few articles on The President before he went to jail, but nothing after, and no pictures. Good.

Rachael called Harry, "Blackie got an ID for you. You will be a waiter."

"Tell Blackie he has no imagination," Harry retorted. "I have three paintings he will put on display. If he wants me to talk to this woman, then I need to be an artist. Not a fucking waiter."

"I don't know if he can do that, Harry."

"If he wants me to meet the countess, he will."

Harry gave Rachael the address of The President's studio. As expected, some guys showed up that afternoon to pick up the paintings and give him his pass. JFK was added to the gala as a replacement artist. Another painter suddenly had a prior engagement and could not attend the Arts for the Homeless Benefit Show.

Harry did an internet search on Mienhard Eldinstein which came up next to empty. He was wealthy. He was an antique and art dealer. He was a philanthropist, a fancy way of saying he knew how to hide his business well. Not the type of person that would interest Blackie.

He searched his wife, the Countess Calliope Eldinstein, and found even less details on her life. He thought maybe she was Blackie's real target. Maybe they had crossed paths, and he was obsessed with her. *Not so far-fetched,* Harry mused. He had only seen her picture once and he could not stop thinking of her.

In his search he found a multitude of pictures of her. Not one of her alone. Meinhard was always there. *His big, fat face with that twisted evil smirk*, Harry reconsidered, *maybe he is the sort of person Blackie is interested in.*

The Countess, not only was she never alone, but she was also never happy in the pictures. He spent hours looking at them and no matter what the occasion, she looked detached. Physically, she was there. In most pictures her hand resting on his arm. But she was a million miles away. Her expression was like stone and her eyes were blanks. But even in that mannequin state she had a beauty that shone through.

Jonathan used to tell him, "A true artist captures the soul of his subject, be it with paint or the camera." It would seem that many artists tried to capture her soul. The sheer volume of photographs that appeared on his computer attested to the facts.

Harry dressed in a tapered tux the night of the benefit, picked out by Rachael. She wore a cherry-red sequined gown with a plunging V neckline. Her golden cleavage accented by a teardrop diamond. Diamonds dripped from her earlobes and did a tantalizing hide-and-seek with her raven's black under-flip curls. Men of all ages and incomes were intrigued by her. Her nine square foot face adorned the gallery wall, and she reveled in the notoriety. Even Mienhard took notice a time or two when she imitated the puckered lips pose for the cameras.

Harry never gave her a second thought. He was circling the galleria like a shark stalking a baby seal, searching for the opportunity to strike. The Countess was more stunning in person. He could hardly take his eyes off of her. True to form, she stood by Mienhard's side, a hand on his arm as if she would drift away except for this great anchor keeping her firmly in place.

Many people, men and women alike, approached the

couple with phony platitudes and overblown overtures. Mienhard had set himself in the middle of the gallery where his lovely wife would make him the center of attention. A place he knew well.

A young waiter balancing a tray of assorted drinks turned and stumbled. His tray unbalanced for a second, long enough to spread a rainbow across Mienhard Eldinstein's white shirt and black tuxedo jacket. Mienhard immediately exploded in a German tantrum bringing security and benefit promoters running. They hustled the waiter from the hall.

"We go now!" Mienhard ordered Calliope.

"Why? You have four other tuxedoes in the car. Go change. I want to stay for the auction," defied Calliope, taking advantage of the situation.

As all eyes were upon him, Mienhard capitulated to her demands and left with his bodyguard. The room returned to the low din of polite conversation.

"You know you probably got that poor boy fired… Mister?"

"Jonathan Franklin Kurkman," Harry turned, introducing himself with two champagne glasses in hand. "Was I that obvious?"

"You've been watching me the whole night. You could have just introduced yourself, Mr. Jonathan Franklin…"

"Just call me, Johnny Boy. That's what my friends call me."

Calliope ignored his offer of champagne. "So, now we are friends. I don't think so. That poor boy is not only going to lose his job tonight, but my husband's men will also beat him up. And if you are not careful, you will be next on the list, Johnny Boy."

"So… We are friends," Harry said with a big smile, "it will make the beating tolerable."

Calliope smiled, "If that is what you're into. But we are not friends, we have nothing in common."

Harry was mesmerized by her smile. This was the first

time he had seen it. Maybe the first time anyone had, "Beautiful."

"I beg your pardon?"

"Your smile… It is beautiful," Harry said absent-mindedly. "We have more in common than you know. We are both prisoners. You of your husband…"

"How dare you." The smile disappeared. "And I suppose you are a prisoner of your girlfriend in the red over there. That is her picture on the wall, and the one over there is you." Calliope pointed over his left shoulder and took one of the glasses from his hand. "A word of advice, Johnny Boy, if you want to pick up a woman, don't bring your girlfriend along."

Harry felt incredibly small. She was right. Rachael invited herself, as she usually did. And why had he brought that picture of her? But he could not concern himself with that now, Mienhard and his goons would be back soon. "I'm not trying to pick you up. I want to paint you. It's an offer I think best made not in front of your jailer. Or I will end up in the alley with the waiter."

"You are no painter, Johnny Boy," she told him. "My jailer, as you call him, is an art collector. And I have been around many artists. Painters smell of colors, oils and dyes, of earth and chemicals. I don't know what type of artist you are, probably a con artist, but definitely not a painter."

"Ouch," said Harry, clutching his heart.

"You probably never held a paintbrush in your life," Calliope declared, taking his hand from his chest and turning the palm up.

Harry's heart stopped beating. Electricity raced from her fingertips up his arm and exploded within his head. All thoughts wiped clean from his mind. The soft touch of her hand was enough to freeze time.

Calliope felt something like a ricochet bullet striking her heart. But instead of killing her on the spot, it brought instant life into her body. A tsunami rose up and swept away the past. It roared back to her, bringing emotions she had long forgotten. They burst forth from her eyes, irradiating Harry in a nuclear blast. She jerked her hand away from his and stumbled backward.

Harry stepped forward but stopped short of a second touch. The power in her eyes, the intoxication of her smile, was more than he could handle. Another touch and he would surely be turned into a golden statue. Thus, the magic she possessed. "Here. Take my card. Call me… Email me… You need not pose in person," Harry struggled to get his words out as he held out the business card. "Perhaps you can send a photo."

"Is that how you painted your self-portrait?" She gazed at the little white card for a minute. "Do you think my jailer would let me go back to my cell with contraband? But, I would like to have a closer look at your work. Don't worry, I'll stay clear of your girlfriend." Calliope had been watching Rachael, who positioned herself in a direct line of sight of them. "By the way, another bit of advice, no one will find you when they search for JFK. I would change the name of the website."

"Thanks, I'll keep that in mind," he said, returning the business card to his pocket, "here comes your jailer."

"Then you'd better get out of here," she warned.

"If I leave now, I will definitely end up in the alley with the waiter."

Mienhard returned and held out his arm. Calliope hesitated just long enough to irritate him then took his arm. Harry introduced himself as an artist with the benefit. Mienhard dismissed him rudely and questioned Calliope relentlessly in German and French.

Finally, Calliope said, "He wants what all the artists I have met want. He wants to paint my portrait."

"He has no talent," Mienhard was quick to judge.

"I'm sure he, like all the others, has enough talent for the picture he wants to paint," she said, taking a well-timed jab at his jealousy bone. Then she realized that it might be bad for Johnny Boy. "You seemed to be interested in one of his portraits or was it just his model that caught your eye?" Calliope accused and abruptly walked across the floor.

Mienhard followed her, furiously cursing in both German and French under his breath.

Calliope stopped in front of the middle of the three paintings. "You will buy this one."

Mienhard looked over the painting, a kaleidoscope of blue butterflies following a white moth in the night sky. He looked at the signature in the corner, "JFK". He read his bio on the podium before the picture, then objected, "This man is a nobody."

By the end of the night Mienhard Eldinstein angrily paid three hundred thousand dollars for 'The Moth'.

Mienhard was still fuming over his wife's disobedience as the sun rose over Central Park. He paced the floor of his apartment in the luxurious 17 Central Park West. The gleaming white limestone rose to meet the sunshine. The ten-million-dollar three-bedroom apartment on the 17th floor was one floor directly above Calliope's twelve-million-dollar two-bedroom apartment. There were private stairs he had built connecting the two through their kitchens. He had been down those stairs five times last night and once again this morning, but she had dead-bolted her door.

The rooms beyond the main one were cut off by the hallway door. There was no access to the back of her apartment. She was safe from his rage for now, and he had business to attend downtown. He set it in his mind to punish her when he returned.

At 8:05 the phone rang. Mienhard gave the driver a ten-minute tirade for being five minutes late even though he could see the accident which snarled traffic along 8th Avenue. He sat in the back seat and ranted about how the driver's tardiness put his whole business in jeopardy. The driver, who had already worked for him for ten years, could only reply, "My apologies, sir."

"This will be deducted from your pay," Mienhard assured him at the end of the next rant. Between outburst he thought about the countess, her resilience, and resurgence of her spirit. He hadn't seen her that forceful in years. It must have been the painter. He would have a man look into his background and perhaps pay him a visit. *Yes, definitely, someone will pay him a visit. And the Countess will receive a stern punishment, unlike any before, three hundred thousand for trash. For him.*

The car finally arrived at a tenement on the lower east side. The old brick buildings seemed to lean on each other for support. If one brick was to fall, the whole block would cave in. Yet, these buildings had stood for a hundred or two hundred years. In all those years, they had only seen despair. The black Continental was delivering a fresh batch today.

Calliope's phone rang. It was the concierge. She had asked the building staff to alert her when her husband left the building. Robert was on duty, he was good, he had a knack for finding out things, like, if Mr. Eldinstein would be out for a short while or the whole day. Robert hailed a cab for the Countess and Madame Olga. He gave the cabbie the address of Olga's brother in the Bronx and told the women they needn't hurry back. Once the cab was on its way, Calliope said, "Driver, take us to 85 4th street."

"What? Where?" Madam Olga asked with a very worried look, "Contessa, you don't want to do this. No good can come from it."

The cab wove through traffic heading south.

Calliope ignored the protest.

"What do you think Mr. Eldinstein will do if he finds out."

"I do not care," Calliope said firmly, "What more can he do to me? Besides, those pictures were so… So… Expressive."

"But you said he didn't paint them."

"I said I don't think he did," Calliope's mind drifted away, pondering the possibilities. Recalling the moment from last night when her whole world changed. "What if he did? At least, he most definitely inspired them."

The cabbie stopped in front of the three-story brownstone and informed the women that he would keep the meter running.

Calliope looked up to the second floor. She could see splashes of colors behind naked glass. Her hand reached for the door handle. She wasn't aware of her movement until she heard the lock click. Suddenly, everything looked jumbled, disjointed, and dark.

She quickly slammed the door as if to keep a demon out and screamed out in a panic, "DRIVE."

Part 3

Upon her return to Greece, Calliope locked herself away in her study. She worked endlessly on a new novel, The Last Song Of Hope. *The title is too long,* she thought, opening a new file on her computer. Hope had heartily burst forth into her world like a newborn star in the cosmos. Shining brightly amid the twisted cloudy world that was her life.

Madame Olga never left Calliope's side since the cab ride in New York. Mienhard was enraged and it had not subsided. Maybe he had them followed, he had spies everywhere. Was that what had frightened Calliope at the artist's apartment? Did she recognize one of his men on the street, or was it Mienhard lurking in the shadows?

Mienhard banged on the suite door with a closed fist and pushed past Madame Olga when she unlocked the door. Through the sitting room and past the bedroom marched Mienhard. Two men followed him, each holding his end of a flat crate.

"Countess! Countess!" bellowed Mienhard as he stopped at the studio door. "Your painting has arrived."

The two men laid the huge flat wooden box on a table and began to uncrate the painting.

Calliope stood on the opposite side of the table anxiously awaiting the appearance of The Moth. "I want you to hang it over there, Christos, out of direct sunlight." She instructed and pointed to a place across the room.

"I don't know what you are worried about," barked Mienhard as the men lifted the heavy cover off the crate. "It's a worthless piece of garbage."

"Not so," Calliope cooed, "you paid three hundred thousand for it." She brushed away the packing material. Her fingers gently rubbed and felt the oils of the blue butterflies. A dozen butterflies were chasing a white moth high into the night sky. Whereas the blue butterflies were shiny with defined brush strokes. The moth was larger yet dull, appeared to be painted with flat house paint.

"I had your artist looked into…"

"Of course, you did."

"He's a criminal," exploded Mienhard, "went to prison for forgery. And he's a dope addict or drug fiend as well."

"That's a drug addict or dope fiend, but no matter what he did or was, he can paint. He's an artist," Calliope dismissed Mienhard and returned to studying the painting. It was in a rich oak frame which made the black of the night sky appear even darker. She wasn't sure what kind of paint Johnny Boy had used for the sky, but it absorbed the light completely. It was like looking into an abyss. The longer you looked, the deeper it pulled you in.

Christos hung the painting at just the right height, not too high as to cause one to have to look up. Calliope found herself transfixed in front of it for hours, watching the moth desperately trying to escape the darkness that pulled at her, the army of butterflies in pursuit. The painting had a strange effect on her. From the moment she saw it, it calmed her. She hadn't realized how restless her spirit was until she stood before The Moth.

Calliope searched the painting after everyone was gone and found what she knew would be there, his business card. There was a brass plate on the frame with his name, address, and the painting's title. But in the upper right corner of the frame was a sliver of white. She climbed on a chair and picked at it until she pulled the folded business card from beneath the frame. It had his instant messenger address on it.

The Moth offered another benefit, it kept Mienhard away. Maybe it was the thought of having spent all that money on something she actually wanted. Maybe it was the way it restored her spirit that irked him. Whatever The Moth did to him, he couldn't be in the room with it for more than a minute.

It wasn't like he spent a lot of time in her suite; he was hardly ever there. He only came to demand some ridiculous thing from her, and to criticize her writing. Calliope was sure he had poisoned every publisher in Greece as to her work. He constantly told her, her only talent was being beautiful. Like a statue, she was form without substance, a body devoid of life. And if this was true, it was his doing.

When her manuscripts were rejected by foreign publishers as well, she had to face the facts; her romances were tragedies. Like her life, lacking warmth and passion. How could she write a romance when her soul had been ripped out of her so long ago. Love forcibly aborted. No, she did not write romances, as hard as she tried, she wrote horror stories.

Without the blood that would at least have made them acceptable.

Boy King was her medieval story of a young prince who must give up the girl he loves to marry the neighboring kingdom's princess to keep the peace. The other king then uses the prince to kill his father and take over his kingdom. The situation leads to revolt in his kingdom, and the love of his life is killed. The Boy King defeats the king and banishes him and his daughter into the harsh wastelands. He reigns over both kingdoms, alone.

Cage Freedom was the modern story of Regina, a topless dancer, who was only free when she was in her cage dancing. When the music stops, all the pain and sorrow of putting her daughter up for adoption comes rushing back to her. Sixteen years later, Regina was replaced in her cage by her orphaned daughter. The pain of seeing her daughter in the cage was too much, and she died of a broken heart.

But that one touch in the gallery had freed something within her. The Last Song of Hope was full of desire and love. Hope was filled with American music, jazz, blues, and rock and roll when she meets an American saxophone player touring Europe…

That was all she got. Calliope turned the card over and over and over. Then she started typing the address in her browser. A simple form popped up with a box and a blinking cursor in it. She typed:

Are you still interested in painting me.

She erased it. Went to stand before The Moth. Finally, she returned to her computer and typed simply:

Received your painting, thanks. She hit enter and off it went.

The reply was nearly instantaneous. *My pleasure, Countess.*

Calliope stared at the screen. It had to be the middle of the night for him. Was he waiting on her reply? Had he been at his computer waiting for all these weeks?

Harry never went back to the W. 4th St. apartment. He knew Eldinstein's men would be looking for him, as Jonathan Franklin Kurkman. He had one of Blackie's men check up on the land-lady; she could give Eldinstein his true identity. But after Johnny Boy's death, she was riding the white horse fast and hard on the money he gave her. If she was lucid two hours a day, it would be a miracle. Heroine had erased all events of the past month and then some. Harry felt sorry for her. He knew she wasn't long for this world.

To be extra safe, he moved out of his hotel too. He could afford better now, and he needed a place with high-speed internet access and satellite TV. He got a place on the Upper East Side as Mr. Keller, a banker; naturally, his credentials checked out.

His computer started beeping like mad at 4:18 a.m. it could only be Calliope. He had set up the computer to alert him when a message came from her. It wasn't hard; no one else had the address. The auto responder had replied. He waited with blurry eyes and dry mouth. He let out a little yelp when the next message popped up.

Giddy as a schoolboy he read it aloud, "What made you paint this picture?"

Harry thought about a dozen good responses, but decided on the truth, "I don't really know."

He knew if he wanted this to work, he had to be as truthful as possible. "Did you like the self-portrait?"

"Yes. Very nice. But I couldn't have those eyes staring at me. So I went with The Moth, no eyes."

Harry chuckled. He picked The Moth because of its simplicity. If anyone at the gallery asked what it represented, which they did, he could come up with any answer, and it would fit. He didn't know what Johnny Boy was thinking when he painted it, but he knew what it meant to him, and probably what it meant to Calliope.

"Escape, that's what I was thinking when I painted it."

"Escape. I can see that. Yes."

Harry queried further. "Would you like to see some other pictures?"

"Yes. I would love to. But how?" Calliope's question had a little yearning in it that leaped from the monitor. "I looked for a website and found nothing on you, Johnny Boy."

"Thanks to your generosity, I am going to rectify that. The artists at the gallery got a whopping one percent of the sales price. I'll use the money to hire a web designer. But for now, I'll email you some photos, OK?"

A few seconds later Harry's screen read: "Ok. But ones I haven't seen before."

He knew that meant none of Rachael, which was fine since there wasn't another of her in the collection. Harry had spent hours before the show taking photos of the paintings. He attached three to his email, one of a factory worker, another of a little girl on a seesaw, and a field of gold-yellow, orange, and copper-red marigolds. He uploaded the pictures.

Harry programmed the pictures with codes that would create a remote viewer on Calliope's computer. He could go anywhere on her computer, and it would display on his screen. But she wouldn't notice. All she had to do was open one picture in one of his emails. He sent five, each with three or more pictures.

He didn't know which picture she clicked on, but half his screen was now Calliope's desktop. He was in. He started a high speed backup of her hard drive. It would take a few minutes. He sent another message: "Have you given any thought to letting me paint you?"

A few anxious moments passed. Harry began to think he pushed too hard. If she turned off her computer the download would stop.

"YES." Popped up on his half of the screen.

Harry felt a little braver now. "Is that, yes, you thought about it? Or yes, I can paint you?"

Calliope read the questions and her heart pounded. It was racing in her chest. Her hands wet with sweat slipped from the keys. She typed. "YES."

Harry read it. He couldn't believe it. The screen then displayed:

"That's a yes to both. But how are you going to manage it?"

He hadn't thought about that. He was not an artist. He typed: "I'd prefer to do it in person. But if that is too difficult, I can work from a photograph. Send me a couple."

He knew her husband would never let her sit for a portrait. He would take the photos to a real artist and have a picture done. He was pleasantly shocked when he saw her reply.

Calliope nervously typed: "I will sit for you. Give me some time to work it out."

Harry ran a hand through his hair. He could feel the silly grin spreading on his face. It was what he actually wanted. He wanted to be with her. He would tell her the truth; Johnny Boy was dead. This whole thing was an elaborate scheme so he could meet her. He started typing: "What about your husband? He's never far from your side."

"Not true. He often takes business trips, leaving me alone for long periods. So, we will have plenty of times."

A red light on his screen blinked. The drive's backup was completed. But Harry wasn't. "I could come there, but that probably isn't safe for either of us. Better we meet somewhere remote."

"Yes, of course. He doesn't tell me when he's going, but

it's usually soon after one of our little trips. I suspect it will be soon. I will email when and where."

"Text tomorrow at this time. I'll be waiting."

Harry wasn't worried about email exchanges with her. The bug he had installed not only allowed him to download everything from her computer. It also encrypted the information and installed an encryption program for her email. All the emails between the two of them were double encrypted. And transmitted through an invisible VPN.

Harry spent a day going through Calliope's files. He looked for backdoors and hidden files. Went back on her computer looking for a network connection he could exploit, there was none. Nothing that led to Eldinstein.

He spent a couple of days reading her novels. They told a lot about her and her life with Eldinstein, but nothing useful. She was heartbroken and bitter, that was for sure. This guy had stolen her youth, and she desperately wanted to make him pay. But there was also a kindness, a gentleness at the very root of her being that prevented her from exacting revenge on her tormentor.

Harry set up an early morning dialogue, early for him anyway. 4 a.m. every day they traded texts. She told him of the life she had with Mienhard. How he beat her at first, then turned to starvation and mental abuse. She confided she was a prisoner but stopped short of asking for rescue. She didn't have to; he made up his mind to free her. The texts quickly became love letters.

"I can't wait to see your face, to taste your kisses, and hold you in my arms."

"I long for you. My body aches for your touch. I burn deep down inside with the thought of you inside me."

"My heart and soul are yours. My will melts to your desires and passions. I wait impatiently for your love."

A week after the first texts, Harry went to the White Horse. He said, "Your Countess is tucked away behind a firewall, very high and extremely hot. It fried two of my bots already."

Blackie was visibly disappointed, "Harry, I thought you were the best hacker in the business. You telling me, you can't do this?"

"No, of course I can," Harry quickly defended himself. "It will take a little more time. I have to upload the virus in parts."

"My boy, get it done, you don't have that much time."

"It would help if I knew what I was looking for," said Harry. He immediately regretted it.

"What does it matter what you are looking for, if you can't even get in the door?" thundered Blackie.

"Well, I could make a targeted attack," Harry covered. Blackie's look was cold and unyielding. Harry knew no further information was forthcoming. He excused himself and left in a hurry.

Blackie picked up the phone, "Rache, Blackie… I think you need to keep an eye on your boyfriend."

Part 4

Calliope sent a text to Harry.

He's leaving tomorrow. Meet me tomorrow.

Harry replied immediately.

I'm booking a flight. I must see you. Have to talk to you. Where is he going? How long do we have?

Calliope answered.

Not really sure. He never tells me anything. Just, 'pack, we are going here or there'. When I am not going, it's just goodbye. I heard him ordering the pilot to ready the jet. I think he's going back to the States. Good thing you are leaving.

Harry was trying to trace Meinhard's movements, which was extremely difficult when someone had their own plane. His flight plans were sketchy, didn't always go where he said he was going. Harry was sure he was wealthy enough to land where he wanted, and when he wanted. Which made him wonder what he really did to make his money. An art dealer didn't need that kind of secrecy when buying and selling works of art. An art smuggler… now there was a man who would want to cross borders unquestioned. But Harry knew enough nefarious types, and most smugglers did not work in the same line as they operated. Why draw unnecessary scrutiny on yourself?

Harry imagined Meinhard to be smarter than that. What he was doing, the art and humanitarian stuff, was a smokescreen. He looked clean and generous, an upstanding citizen, but Harry got a completely different vibe from him. To Harry, he was cold and calculating; his smile and charm a mirror to hide the true personality behind. From what Calliope told him, Meinhard was an unfeeling monster. He was the type of person capable of unspeakable cruelty. Meinhard was a very dangerous person to cross, indeed.

Definitely not the type of person you should be stepping out with his wife when he was out of town. And he knew he should be listening to his head and not his heart, or the little head in his pants. But better judgment was never his thing. It didn't do him any good before, when he got involved with Rachael, and through her, Blackie. As he prepared to board the plane, he felt history planning to repeat itself.

But this time it was different. His search of Calliope's computer did give him some useful information. He knew when she was on the road. He cross-referenced that information with crimes two weeks before or after and came up with some very interesting results. If he was right, and his gut told him he was, Calliope could be in real danger. He had to warn her. That was what he told himself, but the real reason he was boarding the flight was that he needed to see her. No matter the risk.

Rachael didn't need a warning from Blackie to know Harry had lost his mind as far as the Countess was concerned. He looked like he hadn't slept in a month. He was lost in thought whenever she saw him. And she didn't buy the story that he couldn't get into her computer. Whenever she asked about his progress he got a vague, glazed look, and a silly grin that he didn't realize he was wearing. She knew the look; he used to have it for her.

Rachael was monitoring his account. Since no one was looking for him as himself, he took no precautions to cover his tracks. When she woke up and found out he booked a flight to Greece, she booked the next one. If he had found something and was thinking of double-crossing Blackie, then he really had lost it over this woman. Blackie wouldn't waste one moment taking Harry out. He may not love her, but she loved him too much to let that happen. That was the line she kept telling herself on the flight across the ocean. It was better than that she was madly and crazy jealous of Calliope.

Rachael had a lot to be jealous of, it was one thing to be in competition with a vixen, and there were more than a few women who hated her. But to be in competition with one who didn't even know she had that kind of power over men was so much harder to take. She had watched Calliope all night at the gallery. If she had thrown a few knives into that crowd, there would have been a bloody massacred. The way the men fell over each other to get next to her, Harry included. And she didn't do anything to encourage it. It was all so natural to her. Rachael had a huge problem on her hands, how did she compete with a woman like that?

Harry was hers. Whether he liked it or not, and she was not going to lose him, not to her, not to little Miss Innocence. So here she sat, in a plane on her way to Greece, and not a clue as to why he had gone, or what she was going to do about it when she got there. And to make matters worse, Blackie had called her three times before she took off.

Meinhard's plane passed both of theirs, heading the other way. He didn't know about his wife's emails, or what she was planning to do. If he did, he would have had Harry's flight shot down. Not because he cared for Calliope, but she was his, and nobody touched his things. But presently, he was too preoccupied with his own business to consider that something was going on behind his back. Especially anything concerning his wife, he was blind when it came to her.

He had bigger troubles on his mind; things in New York were getting out of hand. He needed to go get control of the situation before his whole business suffered. This little crisis needed his personal attention. He would have to be at his most charming or he could lose a very important client. Besides, he thought, it would do him good to get away from that house, that woman, and that painting.

He landed at a private airport on Long Island, far away from the city. He had the tail numbers changed before he took off in Greece. His flight was registered as a domestic flight from Texas to New York. No cops or custom agents were there to meet his flight, only his limousine, and three companions. Three men, big and black, carried three hooded women from the plane like ragdolls under their arms. The blacked-out limo made its way down the highway towards the city unimpeded in the predawn hours.

They arrived at the tenement before the street sweepers were cleaning the curbs. The limo pulled into the alley and then into a small garage at the back of the building. The three large, black men met them at the door in the basement having travelled in a separate car. They strapped the three young Asian girls to stretchers and wheeled them into a freight elevator. They pulled the steel doors down and Meinhard, the three large black men, and the three Asian prisoners rode up to the third flood.

Meinhard got out and the rest continued to the next floor.

"Dr. Wu, needless to say, I'm very disappointed in these events," Meinhard told the elderly Chinese man.

"Very sorry, careless worker let one of the girls get hold of some very powerful drugs." The doctor's eyes were careful not to make contact with his boss'. "I thought it was best we discard the product. I would have started fresh, but I knew you have a schedule to maintain."

"You realize I have never had this sort of thing happen in any of my other facilities." Meinhard accented each word slowly and distinctly to underscore his displeasure.

"Yes, Sir," the old man finally locked eyes with Meinhard's, which were as solid as a block of ice. "And it will not happen here again. Both parties have been disposed of in a manner that ensures strict compliance with the rules."

Funny how one thing led to another, Harry thought. Blackie wanted him to investigate Meinhard and that piqued his interest in Blackie too. Not all that BS about his background, Harry couldn't care less if he was IRA, or an ex-cop who skirted justice, or any of the other half-dozen stories he had heard about him. He wanted to know how the hell he got busted, and he was almost certain Blackie had rolled on him.

A scam the size they were running was going to generate a lot of heat. The only way to put out the fire was to throw fresh meat on it. Someone the feds could roast to perfection. Harry had been that sacrificial lamb. He wasn't happy about it, but he knew he was the logical choice; give up the lynchpin and people stop looking for what it held together. What he wanted to know was, how did he tip off the Feds? But more importantly, who?

Harry went cold and ghost-white when he finally wormed his way into the files and found the name Banco Nacional de Peru. Someone had withdrawn money from those accounts before the trace records could be erased by the next backup cycle. It wasn't a mistake, he didn't miss a step, not that he ever thought he had, someone deliberately made the withdrawals early. And like all scams, they were just a house of cards. Pull the wrong one and the whole thing collapses.

What shook Harry to his core was that Rachael was the one on the surveillance video. She withdrew the money. She pulled the card from the bottom of the house. What he dearly wanted to know was why? Did she really want to burn him? Why?

Harry struggled with these questions right up until he got the word from Calliope to meet her. Then, all of that didn't seem to matter anymore. But on a long flight like this, your demons had their way with you. He knew Blackie ordered her to do it. No one made a move without his okay. And she didn't bat an eyelash without his approval or say so.

Blackie had his hooks in everyone. And they were deepest in her. He wanted to believe that Blackie forced her to make the withdrawal to keep him away from his daughter. But he also knew Blackie loved money way more than he did Rachael. It was obvious he didn't want Harry with her, but he wanted that money too. That scam would have run for years if she didn't make that withdrawal.

The scam was nearly perfect. He set up hacks into a couple of banks, created accounts, and transferred money from them. After a couple of transfers from one bank to another, the money would land in some offshore bank account. Then someone would go in and withdraw the money as bearer bonds, real money payable to fictitious people. The bonds would then be cashed and the money was gone. It was nearly perfect; the only hitch was to erase the transfer trail before the final withdrawal. That was where Rachael screwed him. Even in a wide brim hat and dark glasses, he knew it was her on that video.

There was no mistaking her walk. Or her ass. She had the bonds made a day before the backups could be restored, which would have wiped out where the money had come from. Once the Feds had that, they traced it all the way back to his computer repair shop. They raided his shop the second he unlocked the doors. Even though he didn't use a single computer of his own. And although the viruses had been launched from different locales and networks the house of cards landed squarely on his head.

~

By the time the plane landed he hadn't slept an hour and had a massive throbbing headache. He was glad he had sometime before going to meet Calliope. He checked into his hotel and then into the rendezvous hotel. They were being extra careful. She also checked into a different hotel and would meet him only when she was sure she was not being followed.

Harry tailed her, looking for signs she was being followed as she went on a shopping trip with Madame Olga. She didn't know he was there. At some point, Calliope would sneak away from her confidant and bodyguard to meet him at the hotel. He passed by an art store and realized that he didn't have any supplies to paint with. He knew this would raise suspicions. But not as much as if he proved he could not draw a straight line.

He stopped in a camera store, remembering what Johnny Boy had once told him, "a picture captures the moment, and a painting captures the time."

He would take pictures of her and tell her he would paint the portraits from them. He was sure it was unconventional but then he wasn't there to paint her. And he was sure she was not really interested in just sitting. He fought every impulse not to go up to her and grab her right there on the street. The feeling was harder to fight than when he had been completely tied to the needle. Desire was a drug that he just couldn't fight.

She didn't appear to have a tail, so he went into the camera store and asked the clerk to show him her best equipment. He hoped she would help him fight his passion until it was safe to go back out on the street. Then he would return to his hotel and wait for the signal as they planned.

Rachael landed on the island of Rhodes early in the morning. She was a half day behind Harry, but he didn't know she had added herself onto his credit account years ago. As his wife, a simple phone call and she knew exactly which hotel he was staying in. She called the company to dispute a charge and the poor sap at the other end gave her the name of the hotel and room number.

She booked a room down the hall from his using his card. The hotel managers were very helpful, thinking she was there to catch her cheating husband. Everyone loves a good scandal.

She camped out in the room and watched when room service made their deliveries. He had breakfast, lunch and dinner delivered. Every day, for four days, he did not leave the room once. She ordered room service too, and as the days wore on, she ordered more and more expensive stuff, and charged it to his account. At first, she thought the extra charges would get his attention and he would come to investigate what she was doing there.

After the third day she was pissed. He had come all the way to Greece just to shack up with this woman. She had a good mind to go down the hall and break down the door. Pull every strand of hair from that woman's head. See how captivating he found her when she was bald.

Instead, she left the hotel for a day trip. The concierge told her about a beautiful place where butterflies nested. It was the only place like it in the world according to him. So, she took a taxi to the Petaloudes Valley. Thousands of black and yellow striped Tiger Moths coated the trees in an undulating, living second skin.

Rachael was enraptured in the beauty and gentle nature of the valley. The slight breezes lifted the moths from their perch on the trees in a swirling cloud and redeployed them softly on their bark. The air was filled with the fragrance of the Oriental Sweetgum trees. It was what attracted the moths and held her captive as well. She watched nature's dance of the butterflies over and over until the sun set.

Rachael returned to the hotel ready to call off her vendetta on Calliope. She'd send a discrete message to Harry and find out what he knew before Blackie had both their heads. She stopped at the front desk and asked for a pen and paper.

"I'd like you to deliver this message to Mr. Harry Rankin, and no one else, understood?"

"Yes, Ma'am," replied the young bellhop and off he went.

A few minutes later an unkempt man showed up at the hotel bar. His face was covered in an unflattering layer of stubble. His black hair was wild, and he smelled of booze.

Rachael figured he was on a weeklong binge. "Who the hell are you?"

"You're the one who sent me this note, 'If you want to still be alive tomorrow meet me at the bar, Rache.' I'm Harry Rankin." He said a bit nervously.

"THE HELL YOU ARE," Rachael exploded. "Harry is my husband, and not even in my worst nightmare would I be married to you. So, I'm going to ask you one more time and if you don't tell me the truth you are going back to your room, minus your balls."

"Whoa, lady," the man took a step back. "Harry paid me five grand to come here and just hang out in the room on his credit card. He didn't say anything about an angry wife."

"What's your real name?"

"Sherman," he paused but an evil look from Rachael compelled him to continue, "Sherman Salazar. Look, I have no idea where he is or what he's doing."

"Go back to the room, asshole," she commanded, "and don't let on that you met me."

It wasn't hard for Rachael to figure out that if Sherman Salazar was pretending to be Harry, then Harry was travelling as Salazar. Unfortunately, the only way she was going to be able to track him down now was by calling Blackie. *Damn it, Harry, I hope this bitch is worth it.*

"Hi, Blackie."

"Hello, Rachael. Are you and Harry having a nice little vacation in Rhodes?" Blackie sneered.

Rachael could taste the venom in his words. A huge lump formed in her throat. She couldn't breathe to talk. She forced the words from her frightened mouth, "It isn't like that, Blackie, you know I'm all yours. Harry thought he found a connection, and I suggested we investigate it before bringing it to you. In case it turned out to be nothing."

"Look, Dove," Blackie's voice turned smooth and nurturing, but Rachael knew when he called her Dove he was anything but calm. "I didn't ask you to play detective, or house, or play me for a fool. He gets information and you turn it over to me. GOT IT!"

"Yes, of course, baby. But since we are already here, can you locate a Mr. Sherman Salazar for me, dear," Rachael was trying to be as sweet as sugar but not tip Blackie off that Salazar was someone he should put a hand on now. "He left out of New York about a week ago. Probably one of Meinhard's peons, but Harry is interested in where he went."

"Where's Harry?" demanded Blackie. "I want to talk to him. NOW!"

"Relax," she said firmly, "He's in his room and I'm in mine. I'm not even sure if he is in there now. He may have gone for something to eat. Just call me back when you get the info and we can get out of here tonight."

Rachael hung up before Blackie could ask any more questions or make another demand. She just hoped he got the information and did not send someone to ask questions of Salazar himself. She didn't know where Harry had gone, but she knew Blackie had a worldwide reach. It wouldn't be hard for him to get to Harry before her if he wanted to.

She paced the floor in her room for the next half hour, all kinds of scenarios running through her mind. None of them had a happy outcome for Harry or her. What if he called Harry's room at the hotel and got that drunken moron on the phone? She'd probably catch a bullet in the head without a word of warning. Or worse, be taken back to face Blackie in person. After an eternity went by the phone rang; it was one of Blackie's men.

Rachael didn't recognize the voice. "Salazar flew to Paris. He registered at Rue de la Paix Hotel." The man hung up.

She stood staring at the phone nervously, expecting it to ring again. Thankfully, it did not. She boarded a plane for Paris that night, her vendetta renewed.

Harry sat at the hotel bar nursing a vodka on the rocks. He checked his watch again. Ten minutes later than when he checked it last. And ten minutes later than it was at that time. A florist delivery guy entered the hotel and left a small bouquet of carnations in the lounge. While the Concierge argued with the delivery man over who the flowers were for, Harry took one and walked out of the hotel. He walked down the quiet street under the watchful Eiffel Tower. He looked lost as he doubled back down the same street again. But he was anything but lost. He was carefully checking for a tail.

He arrived at the Le Sept Codet and went to the interior courtyard, where he saw Calliope sitting in a lounge chair sipping a white wine. He sat in a chair across the courtyard from her and placed the carnation on the table. The waiter walked over and he ordered a vodka Collins on the rocks. When the waiter left, Calliope went to the elevator. Harry studied the other patrons in the courtyard, none seemed interested in her exit. When his drink arrived he downed it, left ample money on the waiter's tray, and headed for the elevator.

Another man met him at the elevator, they entered together. The man pressed the third floor and Harry pressed the top floor. Neither spoke. Harry rode to the top floor then walked down to the fourth. He swiped his key card and opened the door. Calliope stood in the center of the living room in a simple white dress with the Eiffel Tower over her left shoulder in the floor to ceiling window. Harry was blind to all but her standing bare feet on the golden-yellow sandalwood floor. The combination of the scented air and her beauty was an aphrodisiac that he could not overcome. His senses were overwhelmed.

The moment the door opened time stopped. Calliope was caught between breath and heartbeat, between want and desire. Never had she seen the look she saw in his eyes. They reached across to the back of her mind, turning all thoughts black and dark. It cast all reason into a void. No sound, no movement, just a strange burning deep inside her, spreading uncontrolled throughout her, producing waves of sweet, delightful sweat to run down her body. She was most aware of it oozing down her legs.

Both had been held at a distance but were unable to part. Slowly, Harry was pulled towards her. As he neared, Calliope unfolded, her skin seemed to open up, her pores waiting receptacles for his love. Their first touch so many months ago had been electric. As his hands cupped her face, she melted into him. Her body molded to his form. He lost control of his muscles, was liquefied by her heat and absorbed in her. Their lips slipped across each other. Parting on command from some unseen power to allow their tongues to meet and entangle.

Hands and fingers slid under clothing and over skins, searching for treasures hidden and secrets awaiting to be revealed. His hands exposed shoulders, creamy soft curves, an augury of delights to come. Hers reached up, gliding over stiffened pectoral muscles that invited raking nails and promised ever hardening muscles to be discovered.

Her dress fell halfway as a quick tug on the zipper exposed the full breast beneath. Her shoulder straps caught in the crook of her elbows to stop the soft white cotton from reaching her feet. Harry swung his hands down around the curve of her buns and lifted her breast to his hungry mouth. Calliope clasped her hands around his head ensuring he'd get his fill of what she had to offer.

Harry sucked hard and greedily on her peachy buttons, and they responded to his desire, growing hard and dark. He went from one to the other, sucking the whole amount into his mouth, then running his tongue around excited areas.

He nibbled on her and Calliope moaned with pleasure. She locked her legs around his back and entrapped him in her arms. She pulled and tore away his shirt and felt his manhood rise up between her legs. It excited her ever more. He carried her to the sofa and laid her down before the picturesque bay windows. Calliope lifted and slipped the dress from her torso laying naked before his eyes.

Harry had his left knee between her legs and his right foot on the floor, there he stood, transfixed and frozen.

"Please Johnny, make love to me," Calliope reached her hand to his face.

He kissed each fingertip as he slowly lowered himself onto her. His weight trapped her, and he felt for her opening. There was an inferno between her legs, and he rubbed her juices around her tiny hole with his index finger. Her body quivered at his touch and a sigh heated his ear. Harry guided his head to her and kissed her deeply. Locked in a kiss, she felt his head parting and spreading her open. She was tight around him and Harry proceeded slowly with gentle pressure.

He knew she was practically a virgin, having only been penetrated once before. She tensed for a moment and then like a great veil had been lifted she granted free passage, and he sank deep inside her. As he reached as far into her as his length allowed, he murmured, "I love you."

Part 5

Calliope got out of the taxi holding her high heels in one hand by the black spaghetti straps and her shawl over her arm. It was 5 am. Her turquoise floral print peasant skirt swept the lobby floor as she headed toward the elevator of the Hotel Opera. The cool marble floors were soothing to her feet. She didn't quite get to the elevator.

"Every night this week!"

"Madame Olga," Calliope was surprised. "Why are you up so early? And waiting in the lobby."

"I'm not up so early," the elder woman scoffed, "I have not been to bed."

"That makes two of us." Calliope giggled.

"I have been worrying about you. And this man—"

"That makes the three of us," Rachael chimed in from a chair in the corner of the lobby.

The two women were startled. Calliope studied the woman's face intently.

"Come now. It's been a while, but surely you remember me from my portrait."

"Oh, yes. You're the woman Johnny painted for the show," Calliope acknowledged quizzically.

"Johnny?" Rachael joined the women in the middle of the lobby. Her bags were still by the chair. She looked neat but had obviously been travelling all night. "Oh, my! You still think he's a painter. My dear, have I got a story to tell you."

"Why should I listen to…" Calliope fumes. "You are naturally jealous and will say anything."

"Who are you?" Madame Olga asked sternly, stepping between Calliope and Rachael. Shielding Calliope from any possible attack.

"Relax, Momma Bear," Rachael smirked. "I'm here to help her before she gets hurt. But I see I may already be too late. I'm Rachael Dove, Harry's… um… I guess ex-girlfriend now. By the way, his real name is Harry Rankin, and he's a thief, a conman, and an excellent lover. But you probably already know that last bit well by now."

"I don't believe a word of it." Calliope had rage in her eyes and voice.

"Well, let me ask you this," Rachael was sympathetic, "has he tried to paint anything? Sketch you. I bet not, Harry can't draw two straight lines."

Calliope's eyes went dull. She reacted like a prize fighter who had just walked into a vicious combination of right cross and left uppercut.

Rachael took her hand, the one still holding her heels, and led her back to the chairs in the lobby. Like an old and dear friend, she said, "sit down here, honey. I didn't mean to shock you, but you need to know who, and what you are dealing with here."

Madame Olga followed the two women to the corner of the lobby. She was not sure how much to trust this woman but wanted to hear what she knew about this painter, or whatever he was. She sat and held Calliope's left hand, preparing to hear the worst.

Rachael did not disappoint them. "Harry is… was my boyfriend for a while. He pulled the same scam on me. Had his friend Johnny paint that portrait of me, I was so in love with him. Still am, I guess. But Harry and his friend were in love with my husband's money and his bank account information." Rachael caught herself. She couldn't expose too much, in case Harry still needed to gain access to Calliope's computer. Blowing Harry's cover may have already doomed Blackie's plan and put her own neck in a noose. Seeing the way Calliope walked in, reason had given way to jealousy.

"I revealed so much about my husband's business and then he robbed him." Rachael sobbed. "I thought he loved me. My husband found out and sent them both to prison, but the damage he did to my life was irreparable. My husband left me with nothing."

"Then why were you at the Gallery?" demanded Calliope angrily, "if he is so evil, why were you helping him? I don't believe you. You take me for a fool. You think you can come in here with your phony tears and pack of lies and I… I… I don't believe you. None of what you're saying is the truth."

"You don't believe me now," Rachael dropped her head in

shame. "You will when you realize he is more interested in your husband's business than your beautiful body." Rachael got up like she had a heavy load on her shoulders. She wearily picked up her suitcase. "Oh, and the reason I helped him at the Gallery… he said he loved me… He'd pull one more con and then we would be together. I'm sorry. I didn't know it was going to be you. I didn't care. He said he loved me."

Harry got out of the taxi in front of his hotel. Two men approached him from either side. They didn't need to flash their badges for him to know they were police. "Mr. Rankin, please come with us."

"Sorry, boys, the name is Salazar, you got the wrong guy," Harry said, quickly assessing they were Americans, and probably out of their jurisdiction.

"Yeah, entering the country under fraudulent conditions, we could be here to arrest you on those charges, but that's a matter for the French police. I'm Detective Allen with Interpol and this gentleman here is Inspector Rutherford out of our London office. And before you walk into your hotel and a couple of Samuel Blackwell's men, I insist you come with us."

A car pulled up behind them and the two men showed Harry into the back seat. Det. Rutherford, a husky fellow with large, scarred hands got in the back with him. He noticed Harry looking at his distorted knuckles, "Relax, mate, I used to be a bit of a Journeyman, before my hands got too mangled."

Harry found himself in an office building in downtown Paris a few minutes later. It didn't look much like a police station, but then again it wasn't supposed to. The room he was in, however, did look like an interrogation room. It was small, with one table and a couple of chairs, plus a small mirror facing him for the cameras, and a door that was probably locked from the outside. Harry wondered how Interpol knew he was in Paris. If they knew Blackie, and Blackie had him on Meinhard's case, then Meinhard was even more dangerous than he thought. In the five nights he had been with Calliope, they shared many things, stories, and good times, but he couldn't find a way to tell her that her husband was laundering money through his charities, especially the orphanages.

There had been several that had burnt down around the world that corresponded to their trips, and Meinhard had stepped in to help get some of those places back on their feet. He suspected Meinhard may have been behind those fires so he could have access to their business, a place to park money that would not be scrutinized. But what could Blackie's interest be? he had yet to figure that out. And now he was sitting in an Interpol office waiting to be grilled until well done.

"Ok, Loverboy, why don't you fill us in on what your boss and his girlfriend want with the Countess Eldinstein?" asked Det. Allen as he came through the door. He was followed by Rutherford.

"Who, Blackie?" Harry played dumb, but he didn't really have to. He was hoping the police would clue him in. "And what girlfriend?"

"Come on, Harry," Allen said exasperated, "you've been diddling around with Eldinstein's wife for a week. Then Rachael Dove has her boyfriend look you up…"

"Boyfriend? Don't you mean father?" Harry laughed, "and here I thought I was going to work you guys for some info. You got your facts half-ass backwards."

Allen and Rutherford took the chairs across from Harry; they looked at each other and laughed. Rutherford looked at Harry and says, "Sammy Blackwell, the bird's father, you do have shite for brains, don't you?"

Allen joined in, "The only DNA those two share; is what he leaves in her on a nightly basis, you dumb fuck."

Harry looked sick. His chin hit his chest as if his neck had snapped. He stared at his hands folded neatly in front of him. His life flashed before his eyes as if he had been in a dark tunnel and just realized the light he saw coming was the train, and it hit him at full speed.

Allen's face dropped, "You really didn't know you were catching sloppy seconds from your boss' table. OK, let me clue you in on a few other tidbits. Like that embezzlement scheme they sent you to jail for was really so Blackie could move terrorist money around. Every time we freeze some organization's account, he backdoors us and moves the funds to another place. Thanks to you, and your code."

"So, the code is still running?"

"Yes, and we want you to move the money to a bank here in Paris," Rutherford told him. "Blackie is coming here. Probably to kill you himself, his men were supposed to grab you today. If you put Sammy B and the money in the same place, where we can grab him, we'll let you go back to banging the Countess' brains out."

"Of course, when Meinhard Eldinstein finds out, and he will, it will be both of your brains on the floor." Allen warned him, "You do know Eldinstein is in the baby farming business."

Harry's eyes were blank. "I don't see the connection between Blackie and Meinhard. My best guess is he will use my program to steal Meinhard's money. He just needs me to find a bank account to exploit."

"Mister, get your head out of the pussy and for God's sake take a look around." Rutherford scolded him. "You are swimming in a cesspool with sharks."

Meinhard Eldinstein was in the study with Anthony Blanchard and his wife, Anne North-Blanchard. He was smiling and sipping tea with the textile industrialist in their 65th Street Penthouse. Anne was berating him and urging her husband to call off the deal they had made.

Anthony calmly said, "Now, dear, all that fussing is not necessary. These things happen in this kind of business. You have to be prepared for some setbacks. Look at the pictures again, these are three beautiful young women, and the men, collegiate athletes, and one is even a soldier. I'm sure there will be a Tiger's caliber offspring in the bunch."

"Again, let me add, these girls come from the finest families in China," Meinhard assured the irate woman. "Young people sometimes make mistakes. Your generosity will keep that single mistake from becoming a horrible family tragedy."

"A tragedy," the forty-year-old woman dressed in a fine body-hugging red silk dress and diamond ensemble declared, "what do you call what happened to Sue Ling? What was it you said? Ah yes, she experienced a misfortune. She committed suicide!"

"As your husband said, there are sometimes setbacks. Even though Miss Ling knew her child was going to a very fine and loving couple, she just couldn't handle the guilt she felt. I have doubled the counseling sessions for these three women. At no cost to you, and I will keep them together for emotional and cultural support. Call it a lesson learned." Meinhard was stroking the woman's shoulder and looking at her with big, puppy-dog eyes.

"What about—" Anthony began.

"You will have the first pick, naturally," Meinhard assured before the white-haired sixty-years old man could completely voice his concern. And before his wife could raise the next obvious question, he added, "I've already lined up two very nice families for the other girls. Black Asians are quite in demand these days."

Meinhard left the Blanchards' satisfied his contract with

them was secure. He went back to the tenement that served as his New York baby farm. The three girls were chained to their beds by one ankle. There was one empty bed in the room. Each of the four apartments on the three upper floors was set up in the same way. They had three bedrooms with four beds, a kitchen where the women's food was prepared, and a living room where they ate. The windows were nailed shut and painted black. All the women were slaves; sold for the purpose of having babies. These three did not resemble the young girls in Meinhard's pictures; he purchased them from a trader in Vietnam. Who might have purchased them from their families or simply cut his costs and kidnapped them. The three black men who would father the babies were the same three men who had taken the girls from the plane, Meinhard's men, and it was part of their job and pay.

"These new girls test clean, yes?"

"Yes, Mr. Eldinstein," replied Dr. Wu, "No drugs in their system. And they appear to be of a good age. I don't foresee any trouble in conceiving or delivering. The men are servicing them nightly. We will be back on track before the month is out."

"By back on track, you mean six months behind," scoffed Meinhard.

His phone rang and his countenance turned increasingly sour. His lips were thin, and his eyes narrowed. "How long has she been gone? And you are just now calling me…Paris… for shopping… Yes, of course, send somebody. But do not make contact, just watch and wait for me to arrive."

"Trouble, Mr. Eldinstein?" the doctor asked.

"Never mind that. Tend to your business here," Meinhard dismissed him.

He was crazy with anger. The incompetents who surround him were pushing him to breaking point. He saw a homeless man sitting at the foot of the bridge holding a sign, 'Will work for food'. He told the driver to stop.

Meinhard got out and stood over the man, "This is not your lucky day, my friend."

Three shots rang out under the bridge.

Harry did what the police asked him to do and left their office. He went straight to Calliope's hotel room, desperate to warn her about Meinhard. The police had filled him in on the true nature of his business. And Harry filled in the missing parts of their investigation into Meinhard, the parts about the orphanages. Baby farming was much more insidious than illegal adoptions.

Meinhard was doing much worse than just selling babies. He burned down those orphanages to cover up the kidnapping of hundreds of children who were then sold into slavery around the world. And the orphanages he built were forced sex camps where the women were impregnated and their children sent off as factory workers to Asia, India, and the Middle East. Or they were sent to work in illegal mines in South Africa and South America. The truly unfortunate ones were born and raised to be boy soldiers in the ever-changing landscape of the African arena. Meinhard Eldinstein was a good ol' slave trader.

Harry banged repeatedly on the door.

The door flew open. "HARRY!"

"WHAT THE HELL ARE YOU DOING HERE?"

"Now, don't be mad, Harry." Rachael walked back into the hotel suite. "Your sweet little Countess let me catch up on my sleep after my long trip and short talk to set the record straight." She passed through the living room back to the bedroom. "I can see why you like her so. She is a sweet, sweet woman."

"RACHAEL! Get out of here!" Harry slammed the door shut. "And put some clothes on first."

Harry paced back and forth. He started for the bedroom several times then fought the urge to go in there and beat her silly. He knew Rachael was toying with him, but he was in no mood for her games. He didn't expect to see her, but since she was there, he needed answers. He had so many questions flying around his head. And he was sure all the answers were going to infuriate him. So, he impatiently waited for her.

"Oh, sorry to make you wait so long, baby. I had to get a shower in after I was sent on that wild-goose-chase to Greece." Rachael was standing in the bedroom doorway in just a long tee shirt that she put on over her wet body. It clung to her and her nipples were just starting to show through. Water dripped from her hair one drop at a time. She saw the anger in him and kept her distance. "What were you thinking, Harry? Taking off like that. I had to finally call Blackie to track you down. He's not happy."

"I don't give a damn about Blackie." Harry looked away. "Or you. And you didn't think I'd know you are tracking my accounts? I taught you how to get added to an account."

"Baby, I know you are mad," Rachael cooed, "You were expecting to find your little princess here. Harry, she's a butterfly and you and me, we're just moths. We kinda look the same, but people instantly adore her. Us, they crush, without a second thought. I still think we are better off, though. I wouldn't want to live my life in a cage. But the Princess, she flew the coop after hearing the truth about you… and me."

"And which truth did you tell her?" demanded Harry, "the one where you and I are lovers working for your mean old father? Or, and get this, I just learned it today. The one where I am a fool and you, and your lover Blackie, have been dicking me in the ass for years. You know, like how much you two must have laughed when you sent me to prison, because I really like that one, Dove."

"All of it is the truth," Rachael sank into a chair, the seductive air about her evaporating before his eyes. She wrapped herself in a cloak of shame and sorrow.

He had never seen her look like this.

"Blackie started out as sort of my father, I don't know who my real father is. I think he left when my mom started doing heroine. Or maybe he's some john my mom did to support her habit. Anyway, she took me into the White Horse Bar one day when I was eight, and I never left."

Paula Dove walked into the White Horse Bar early in the morning. "Blackie, is Christopher around?"

"It's too early for him. Shouldn't your little girl be in school about now?"

"You better be bringing me my money, bitch." The door to the backroom swung open and Christopher LaCorte stood there.

"I have something good for you," Paula said and grabbed Rachael by the hand. She shook badly as she entered the backroom. The door shut.

"Shit!" said Samuel Blackwell as he came from behind the bar.

In the office, Paula sat on Chris' desk, playing with his tie. "Come, baby. You know I'll get the money. I haven't been able to work because I been sick."

"You owe me three hundred already," Chris slapped her hand away. "There was a time you could make it in a night, but now, not even in a week."

"Look, just give me something to get me straight," Paula pleaded, "I'll leave the girl here with you until I come back with your money. Look how pretty she is."

Rachael was on the sofa and Paula sat beside her; she helped her mother tie off a vein in her arm. Paula shot up and dropped her head back. After a couple of minutes, she was back,

"Now, you go be nice to Mr. Chris, baby. You do whatever he wants you to do. It's all right."

"Come on over here, little girl. Let your mommy sleep. I have a game I want you to play."

Blackie burst through the door. "Why doesn't she come out front with me? She can sweep up while you take care of your business with Paula."

"My business doesn't include you," Chris said, getting to his feet. He pushed Blackie towards the door. Blackie was younger but much larger than his boss. One of the reasons he hired him. "She owes me four hundred dollars now. Look at her; you think SHE'S worth four hundred dollars?"

Blackie looked over at Paula sprawled on the sofa with a needle in her hand, then at Rachael's big bright eyes. "I'll pay you what she owes. But you stop giving her the stuff. Let her get clean."

"Oh. So, you are going to pay me, with my money. This is my bar, my business, and you work for me."

"Not anymore." Blackie pulled out a gun and shot him in the face at point blank range.

"That was the first time I saw him kill someone," Rachael looked up. Tears streamed down her face. She was wiping her eyes with the back of her hands. "It wasn't the last. He broke some guy's neck for touching me in the bar one night. He treated me like his daughter, protected me. Until the day you walked into the bar. I was sixteen. Blackie saw how I looked at you, and he called my mother's bill due. He stopped being my father and like it or not made himself my lover."

"So… What? Now, it's my fault I went to jail for seven years?" Harry was a little sympathetic but still mad.

"The day I walked into that bank was the day I saved your

life," Rachael said angrily. "I got you sent to jail. Blackie was going to send you to your grave when he was through with you, Harry. He had your code and knew how to use it. He didn't need you anymore. But I did."

He then told her of the Interpol plan to arrest Blackie in the bank tomorrow. He didn't know why, but he warned her to stay away from there. They were after Blackie, not her, and not him. He said his goodbyes, from across the room, she was still too hot to handle. *Kryptonite Eyes*. He was sure it was the last time he was looking into them.

He knew where Calliope might have gone. He had to get to her before anyone else figured it out. The next morning on the train platform Blackie was on TV being led out of the bank in handcuffs. He shook his head sadly when he saw Rachael Dove coming out of the bank behind him in cuffs. What the hell was she doing there? She couldn't protect him from Blackie. He had to know he had given the police the accounts. Maybe she thought if she was there Blackie wouldn't suspect him. After all, he would never put Rache in harm's way. He figured it was her way of atoning for the trouble she had caused him. Trouble he hoped he could undo now.

Meinhard got word that Calliope had left Paris. He ordered the pilot to change course to the south of Bourgogne, her family home, but knew it was too late for him to head her off. He ordered his men to stop her before she reached the farm. He made it clear no harm was to come to her, but she was never to set foot on that property, even if they had to burn down the farmhouse.

Harry knew Calliope had no place left to go. Even though she had hated her life in the House of Rancid Grapes that was where she would be headed. She was a couple of hours ahead of him and travelling by car. He could never catch her in time. He feared what she would find there. What would happen to her if she showed up unannounced and uninvited?

He called Det. Allen, "You have to stop Calliope from going to her house."

"Why? What's waiting for her back in Greece?" asked Det. Allen.

"No, not Greece," Harry rubbed his forehead, "not that house, the family farmhouse. She has no idea what is waiting for her there."

"Ok. Give me a plate number and I'll put out an APB on the car."

"Sorry, I don't have that information," Harry apologized. "Throw up a dragnet or something."

"Just like that, just because you say so," Det. Allen railed, "You have to give me more to go on than that."

"Let's just say bad things are going on there. I don't think she needs to see it."

A motorcycle cop pulled Calliope's car over. He detained the pair of women. The police pulled over four cars in all on the road outside the farm. Three going to the farm and one leaving, the one leaving had two men and a baby less than a week old in it. They were detained. One of the other two cars, which were heading to the farm, had two young girls, both drugged. The two men in the car were immediately placed under arrest. The last car, Calliope and Madame Olga saw pulled over contained four roguish men. All armed, and the car had a trunk filled with full gas containers. They were arrested on weapon charges.

Calliope was taken to the local police station in shock, where they would tell her nothing of the goings-on at her family vineyards. Her father rarely went to town, and her brothers were their usual troublesome selves. They hadn't made much wine in the years that she'd been gone. Not that that was a bad thing, joked one of the older officers who knew her well. He told her they had received a call from Interpol to stop all traffic in or out of the place, and specially, take her into protective custody.

Meinhard's jet circled the vineyard once as the pilot looked for a clear stretch of road to put down on. As he got close to the one road that ran straight to the farmhouse, he saw the grapevines were dry and dead. Although the road wasn't wide enough to accommodate the plane, the dead vineyard posed no threat and offered no resistance to its landing. The jet's wings snapped the vines in half as it mowed to a stop, a few hundred feet from the house.

He argued with the pilot for several minutes when he was told that taking off from the field would be impossible. Then, he exited the plane angrily and walked up the dirt road to the farmhouse. He was too enraged to notice that no one had come out to question his landing in the field. On the plane he had received one report after another about Calliope and some man in Paris. If she thought he'd just let her run off like some starry-eyed schoolgirl, he had plans to teach her different. And her father and brothers had better not try to stop him if they wanted to stay in business.

He barged into the house bellowing, "Countess… Countess…. Come to me this instant. Ameri, where is that girl?"

He waited for a moment. He listened. The house was deathly silent. There should be a dozen or more girls here now, at least three or four babies born and being prepared for delivery. He shouted, "Wine maker, you can't even handle producing a few children. I will have to send someone to take over the operation from you, you drunken idiot. And where are your moronic sons? do not tell me they cannot handle a few sex slaves." He proceeded through the house, going from one room to the next until he reached the kitchen at the back of the house.

Ameri sat at the same old table where he had sold his daughter years ago. His hands folder neatly in front of him, handcuffed together. The two sons were seated next to each other, also in handcuffs. There were six French policemen in black combat gear pointing Uzis at their heads.

Det. Allen stood behind Ameri with a hand on his shoulder, "Ah, Mr. Meinhard Eldinstein, won't you join us. Please take a seat."

Meinhard turned to run. Det. Rutherford caught him square in the face with a fast and powerful right hook.

Meinhard's head snapped backwards, taking his body with it to the kitchen floor.

"I was hoping you'd do that, you slimy bastard." Det. Rutherford stood in a fighter's stance, waiting for Meinhard to get up. Hoping he'd make a go of it again.

Meinhard lay back down and wiped the blood pouring from his nose on his sleeve.

"Men, put that lump of shit in the chair there," Allen said, pointing to the other end of the table. "Just so you know, these three assholes already confessed. The kidnappings, the rapes, the baby selling, all of it and they named you as the mastermind behind the operation. And with your little outburst..." Allen played back Meinhard's words. "You'll be someone's SEX SLAVE for the rest of your life."

Harry arrived at the police station in a squad car. They picked him up from the train station. TV News stations were already covering the sensational story that unfolded out at Calliope's farmhouse. He stood quietly by the door and watched the look of satisfaction growing on Calliope's face as she watched Meinhard, her father, and her brothers being led to the police van on a chain. He said softly, "I'm so glad the police were able to get to you in time."

She turned to him, her face a kaleidoscope of emotions. She was relieved to see him, mad at him for all the lies, happy that he was safe, and totally in love with him despite everything. "I saw Rachael was taken into custody earlier, was that yours doing also?"

"I tried to warn her," Harry said with a hint of despair in his voice, "but she was in too deep, I guess. All those thing she told you, whatever she told you, it was probably pretty close to the truth."

"I know what the truth is, and what is not," Calliope took hold of Harry's face and kissed him gently, trying to ease his pain. "I told you the day I met you, I knew you were no artist, at least not a painter. And I knew right then that I loved you and I could see that you loved me. You had the same look in your eyes that Johnny Boy captured in your portrait."

"Johnny Boy tried to teach me to paint once," Harry kissed her long and hard. "I think I'm ready to give it a try. I have the perfect subject."

"Who? Me? I don't want you to paint me," objected Calliope, "I have been an art object long enough."

"Oh… No... Not you, my dear. I know a little island in the Caribbean that has the most beautiful species of moths living there. Besides, I couldn't take those eyes staring at me all the time."

THE END

MOONBEAM

I am Samuel Sinner. Yes, that Sam Sinner, Professor Moonbeam, Doctor Energy, Mr. Fusion, Sir E-lectricity. I know you all heard of me. How I saved the world. Brought us out of the darkness. It's what you've all read on the new internet.

But that is not the whole story. It's not even half of the truth. Yes, most of the story came from me. Okay, all of the stories came from me. Truth be told, I had to leave the best part, the before the darkness part—the how and why of the crash—out. Not because I didn't want to take credit, or more accurately, blame for what happened. If I'd made it known what my plans were before I did it, OPEC, US Auto, and any number of powerful forces would have stopped me. I'm not talking about lawsuits and legal injunctions. No, I'm saying bullet in the head, buried in the desert, never heard of or from again.

This is not me being melodramatic or some lame attempt to justify a bad idea. The idea was good, as we all know now. But in 2030 to declare I was going to give the world unlimited free energy, that would not go over well. Let's take a step back, ever since Benjamin Franklin and Thomas Edison figured out how to use it, Edison more than Franklin, electrifying the world has been the Holy Grail of power.

Energy built empires. The lack of, or the inability to maintain that energy led to their downfall. Energy has never been clean, cheap, or free. But the world was in bad shape, and the scientists and engineers were stuck in the $E = MC^2$ box. Fusion power was the answer, but cold fusion, hot fusion, small fusion, or big fusion was unattainable inside the box.

Okay, the first truth, I am not a great scientist as all the stories say. I am not even a good engineer. I finished at the bottom of my class. My PhD, the Nobel, all of it was given to me after my success, not because of it. However, I had a hunch the reason why the tokamak, stellarator, and z-pinch reactors failed to maintain fusion was that they were being operated here on Earth. I figured the interference from Earth's magnetic field coupled with the force of gravity was the box. If the reactor operated outside Earth's influences, it could be sustainable.

Of course, there was the problem of treaties banning nuclear programs in space. I considered this as a ban on weapons, not reactors. Many satellites use nuclear reactors for power. Still, for the afore-mentioned reasons, I kept my work a secret.

As I said, I am not the best engineer, but I was able to take the best parts of the reactors' designs and came up with Sunspot. A bit of a misnomer because sunspots are dark. Now, I think it is safe to say, I raised money to build Sunspot by crowdfunding on the internet. Naturally, I couldn't truthfully say what the money was for, but a few good stories about cancer victims, lost pets, and other heart-tugging tales did the trick.

Also, I kept the cost down by making Sunspot small. Really Small. The size of a six-pack beer cooler. It was the one I took to the beach on weekends. The fusion power was generated by using lasers in the six beer cans to raise the temperature and density of the hydrogen plasma. The most expensive parts were the super magnetics needed for containment and the cooling system.

Did I say I am not a true engineer? I am good at using the internet to find the correct time and place to launch Sunspot. And to acquire, let's say, surplus rocket equipment. Since the Sunspot and its controls were so small I only needed a two-stage booster. The first stage I built out of carbon fiber and a fuel mixture from MIT. The second stage needed to be a little more robust. At the time, I wasn't as concerned with governments knowing I was launching a rocket. Getting clearance from the US or any other country was cumbersome. Everyone wanted to inspect the payload, and that wasn't going to happen.

Truth number two. Unlike the popular saying about mice, the first mouse gets the cheese and eats all the other mice. So, I wasn't going to let some government bureaucracy tie up my plans while they stole and implemented it for themselves. NASA's website pinpointed the perfect window, the week of June 22, 2032, in the Caribbean Sea.

I rented a fishing trawler from a company north of Miami. They probably thought I was a drug smuggler because I didn't have a merchant marine license. They were glad to accept three times the standard fee – in cash. I launched at noon on the 24th.

The first stage took off slow from a floating platform I towed a half mile behind the trawler, just south of Cuba. Sunspot eased into the sky atop a glowing golden tower of flames as to not damage the delicate instruments. Then quickly rose to Mach 1.4 in thirty seconds and continued to climb for another two minutes. The radio in the wheelhouse squawked in English, Spanish, and other languages as it scanned the bandwidths. Multiple countries expressed concerns with the rocket as it arched eastward. None more than a United States naval vessel acknowledging it had tracking and getting a weapon's lock. The AIM-9 rocket engine fired. The Sidewinder's second stage kicked Sunspot to Mach 2.5 and seconds later it was out of range and in space.

I had to modify the upper part of the Sidewinder to take Sunspot to the Lagrange 4 point. I cut small holes in the body of the solid fuel booster rocket to push the reactor to the proper place. The nose cone blew apart from compressed air and put the reactor into a halo orbit sixty degrees ahead of the Earth. I returned the boat then went home to my headquarters in the Adirondack mountains of New York. The telemetry data was green. The reactor was right where I wanted it. There were no gravitational forces and minimum electro-magnetic energy, which the reactor was shielded against. On July Fourth, 2032, one minute past midnight, I fired up Sunspot.

I was confident of success but prepared for the fireworks show of a lifetime. The former happened and Sunspot's data link reported massive energy levels. Okay, I am sure everyone wants to know how Sunspot works. Like the sun, it takes hydrogen and fuses it into helium. Basic fusion. Multiple lasers in the mirror cylinder chamber converge on the hydrogen atoms to replicate conditions at the sun's core. But unlike the sun, it does not have a large supply of hydrogen. So, after the fusion process takes place, some of the energy is used to fission the helium. More energy is generated. And then the process repeats. Plasma is in a constant state of fusion and fission. The magnetic containment held it steady. So, from a relatively small amount of solar energy to start the cycle, millions of megajoules are produced.

The usable power was off the charts. To say I was proud of myself would have been the biggest understatement of all time.

I let Sunspot run for a month. The excess energy fed the magnetic containment making it stronger than it needed to be. Sunspot was spinning like a top. Figuratively, of course, or literally internally, as I watched the data feeds. I thought about my announcement to an energy hungry world. I'd be a superhero, bringing clean, free, unlimited energy to Earth. Just one last test to run.

Truth number three. Sometimes knowing the numbers beforehand can prevent unexpected results afterwards. I had a microwave laser (a maser) attached to the reactor. Sending the energy to receiving stations on Earth in microwave pulses was the plan. But there were no stations deployed, and I had to know how much energy I could send. I decided to fire the maser at a safe target, the Moon.

For a brief moment, I considered using the maser to write my name on the moon's surface. I programmed the maser to burn the letters several miles long and wide making my name visible from Earth. But that would be the act of a supervillain not a hero.

In hindsight, I made the right decision. I trained my telescope on the spot. Fired the maser. Moments later a small cloud rose from the moon's surface. The maser blasted a half-mile crater one hundred feet deep.

Almost immediately, alarms in my office sounded. I lost signals from multiple sources. My heart stopped and a rock of dread formed in my gut. I ran downstairs in time to see a cascading failure of lights going across the Adirondacks. Now, I am no physicist, but I knew a massive EMP hit the world. An electro-magnetic pulse, the thing that fries electrical equipment. Sunspot suffered a major malfunction. The sky lit up with blue, green, red, and orange streaks racing from east to west. Fragmented bolts of electrical energy wrapped around the world. An eerie glow of the Aurora Borealis lingered overhead.

Back in my office, the data stream from the reactor confirmed firing the maser caused a substantial drop in the containment field. Sunspot recovered but the EMP that radiated from it took out every satellite in orbit and major power station on the planet. We were in a total blackout.

My diesel generator kicked in, quietly restoring power to my mountaintop home. I watched the sporadic dots of light from the mountainside to the valleys do the same. Most communication channels were down. Television and radio were nothing but static. Telephone and cellular were dead too. The internet completely cleared. There wasn't even a '404 page not found' message. I picked up crackling shortwave and ham radio.

What I heard was pure panic. Planes landed without tower controls. The planes themselves were fully operational due to the Faraday effect, but they got no help from the ground on which runways were clear. They had to wait to get close enough to see and make a quick decision on putting the aircraft down or going around again. A lot of what I heard was militaries threatening to strike whoever was responsible for this attack. The militaries knew they were transmitting over open channels. The world was on the brink of World War III.

Truth number four. If they cannot prove it, you did not do it. Or, don't ask for forgiveness until you fix what you broke. The data from Sunspot showed I should've had a little external force to keep the containment field in place. I built the full-size version of Sunspot, and it sat on the launchpad in my silo ready to go. Yes, the place I bought in New York was a decommissioned ICBM site. How could I afford all this? You'd be surprised how generous people are to a three-legged, one-blind-eyed dog that needs heart surgery.

I quickly recalculated what it would take to land the fusion reactor, which was built out of my minivan, on the moon. I reduced some of the shielding and added wheels to the twelve maser generators that needed to extend from the van. I figured in the gravitational effects of the moon to regulate the power fluctuations necessary for the reactor. I renamed Sunspot II to Moonbeam. Two days later Moonbeam was ready to go.

Without NASA or the internet, I hadn't a clue where any of the dead satellites were. An unknown number started falling out of orbit and burning up in the atmosphere. All planes were grounded so that was one for my side. I waited a week until the white vapor trails of dead satellites went down to one per hour.

I could not wait any longer. Troops amassed on borders and nervous fingers danced around the nuclear buttons. Only the lack of information kept the missiles in their silos. I double-checked my numbers, once bitten twice shy, and launched Moonbeam. I prayed the launch wasn't mistaken for a nuclear strike by one of America's enemies. But the lack of satellite warning systems gave a good chance it would go unnoticed. Moonbeam would take three days to land on the moon. The next day I launched Skypad, the orbital receiver, and on the third I moved my yacht into New York's harbor. That night, Moonbeam fired a yottajoule of energy at Skypad. Skypad stored most of it and transmitted the rest to my yacht, The Steel Breeze. The Steel Breeze brought New York City back to life.

As you know, on September 1, 2032, I addressed the United Nations. Amid boisterous accusations and hurtful name-calling, I informed the world that a massive EMP from Sunspot caused a worldwide blackout. Everyone believed I was talking about a natural occurrence. Half-truth is the better half of a lie. Plus, given my low credentials as a scientist and engineer no one thought I could be behind such a catastrophe. Then I promised to power anyone who built receivers for free. I detailed how a network of satellites and earth-based receivers would power the world. A group of scientists and engineers improved my designs for the satellites and ground-based receivers, and the world's nations adopted my plan.

You may say, I could have avoided all of this if I went to real scientists and engineers in the first place. But I will tell you that my little six-pack beer cooler reactor did exactly what it was designed to do. It proved me right, and wrong. Imagine the consequences if I had fired up Moonbeam in open space. The EMP would've been a quad-zillion times more powerful. I know that's not a real number, but the effects could very well have electrified the entire atmosphere. And electrocuted every living thing on the planet. So, Sunspot did its job. And because I was a hero, no one needed to know the little details. I vented the hydrogen gas from Sunspot, pushing it out of orbit and towards the sun. It took years to fall into the sun but the last telemetry from Sunspot came as it crossed the orbit of Mercury. It lived up to its name as a tiny spot on the face of the gigantic Sun before it melted away.

The next eight years, you know. I didn't solve all the world's problems; I just made it a little cleaner place to live. Well, that's the story. This is the only time you will hear from me. And if anyone tries to use this story against me, let me just tell you the last truth. Everything you read on the new internet is fake news and conspiracy theories.

THE END

THE PATH TO FREEDOM

This was going to be an unusual day; Pappi woke me before the sun. I was not expecting that, being Sunday and all. I thought I had my days mixed again. I often did, not having to work the fields yet, but next year, when I turn thirteen, I'll join Pappi, Isaac, and Nate working the tobacci. My chores were feeding the chickens, goats, and pigs, and they never rose before the sun.

Pappi shook my shoulder and whispered, "Get the hickory rods and lines. We are going down to the creek and catch some fish. Be quiet. Don't wake your brothers and sister."

I peeked across the shanty, the light of the embers in the hearth painted their faces. I rolled from my straw-stuffed mat and blanket and stretched. I grabbed two long hickory poles and a roll of twine. I carefully picked up a couple of sharpened bone hooks and dropped them in a tobbaci sack. Momma was still sleeping in her bed near the door; Pappi had already gone outside.

I looked around, there was not a hint of dawn on the horizon. A strange start to the day indeed. Pappi placed a hand on my shoulder and squeezed, a sign to pay close attention to what he was about to say. He had a way, a look, or an act, which meant you needed to commit what he said next to memory and never hesitate in the re-telling.

"Now, listen here, John."

This was serious. He always called me by my family name when he was serious, instead of Sonny. My eyes widened.

"No need to worry, boy. Just remember, if anyone asks, we went down to the creek to catch catfish. Everybody knows cats bite best before the dawn. And, no matter who asks, Momma, Sara, the boys, and especially Master Stephen, we went fishing."

I nodded and followed him down the road towards the creek.

He carried a lantern but didn't light it. Not that we needed light to follow the path, but the light would scare away the black snakes. Momma always told me not to walk in the dark because one bite from a black snake could kill; even a baby had enough venom in its bite to kill a boy my size. But Pappi was smart, he knew that only the black snakes that lived near the creek were biters, he thumped the ground with his walking stick. Any snake would crawl from the path before we reached it. I did not know how far from the creek the really dangerous ones traveled; I thumped the ground with the fishing rods. Just to be sure.

We passed the broken tree that looked like an A. I was never allowed to call it that since I wasn't supposed to know my letters. Master Stephen had taught me some letters and numbers too. He said it was the only way I could properly play the game, Hide and Seek. He made me swear a death oath not to tell Master Charles or we'd both be whipped.

The path under the A tree led to the pool in the creek which was the best place for catching cats. We were a half mile past it before we went down an un-trotted embankment. Then we walked on the stony shore a bit longer. The sun was just rising when my father sat me on a thick branch over the water. He put a couple of rocks in the sack.

"If you hear or see anyone heading this way, you throw a rock into the water. And if anyone asks what you are doing, remember you are catfishing. I am off in the woods that way," he pointed up the creek from where we came, "getting more worms for bait."

I nodded and he headed downstream and around the bend. I tied a hook to the twine and measured an ample length, so the hook rested on the bottom. I tied the end to the pole and waited. I was a good cat-fisher, but I didn't think I'd catch any with a bare hook.

The sun was peeking above the treetops when Pappi returned with a sack of four catfish. He helped me from the branch and handed me the sack. "You did good today, Sonny. Pull in four nice-sized cats, right?"

"Yes, Pappi. They put up a fight, but I got them alright."

We walked the shoreline back to the path to the A tree then back up the path to our place.

We stood in front of the big house, Sunday Service had just begun for us. Master Stephen Godwin was sitting in his father's rocker, which was now his since Charles Godwin had passed on seven years ago. Old Master, what most called him, had increased the farm to fifty acres and bought twenty field hands to work it. Peaceful Plantation had stretched all the way to the creek when he was alive. The big house looked better then, too, every year we all put on a fresh coat of white paint and trimmed the doors and windows in sunshine yellow.

But the creek was shrinking, and they sold bits and pieces

of the Plantation to where it ended at the Deep Corner where we lived. The Deep Corner wasn't much good for planting, the ground was hard most of the time and filled with water every rain. Our quarters were built on long logs to keep them dry. During the rainy season, the water would cause the logs to shift and if you weren't careful a foot or hand would get crushed between them. Pappi would pack the logs with mud which helped hold them together.

The preacher was in the middle of his sermon when he suddenly stopped. Master Stephen rose out of his rocker like he was possessed by the spirit. It wasn't until Ol' Roy thumped his walking stick next to me that I knew why everything had become so quiet.

"Cotton." Pappi said.

"Abram," Ol' Roy replied. He winked at me and shoved his walking stick into my hand. The walking stick, which he called Albihere, was white oak, as white as his hair. There were faces carved into it, and they began their whisperings. I wasn't sure why, but no one noticed the whisperings but me. And Cotton.

I worked with Ol' Roy feeding the chickens. Cotton, as he preferred to be called, said I had the gift. Every time I saw the walking stick—and I saw it every day—it had a new face. Most were the same but there was always a new one that replaced another. One day I asked him how that could be?

"Albihere shows us those who are important to us now."

"But it is you who carves the faces," I said. I must have been eight years old at the time and was watching him work on the walking stick. It was already covered from end to end and all around with faces. Yet he was still flicking little bits of wood from it.

"I only hold the blade," he said with a wide smile, "the faces come forth on their own."

The reason the congregation went silent was because

Cotton never came to services. We were all made to attend, but no matter how hard the overseers looked they could never find Ol' Roy. In time they just stopped looking. The preacher started up again, and Young Master Stephen slid back into his rocker.

"Abram, what did you hear from the Red Mill's folk?" Cotton asked, barely moving his lips.

"Young Master lost at auction," Pappi's head bowed as he sang his reply in tune with the hymn. "The tobacco crop was sold for less than half what he wanted. It was said he will sell half of us to make up for the loss. Mostly the women and children, I figure."

"Then you go tonight. While the moon is a sliver of itself and at your back." Cotton looked up to the sky. "No clouds, good for the hunted, bad for the hunter. Pass the word, you must all go. No one stays behind."

"There be seven families here, more than forty folks…"

"I know the count." Cotton's voice was strong but low. "It didn't matter to Moses if it was one or one hundred. Besides, anyone who stays will surely suffer the boy's wrath."

"I thought you didn't believe in their religion."

"I do not have to believe the story to understand the message told. You know the plan, bring everyone to the gathering before the moon breaches the treetops."

The families left their shoes—those who had a pair of dried and cracked deerskin moccasins—on the ground outside their cabins. No one wore their shoes inside for fear the smell of tobacco would draw snakes. Each of the cabins had a fire burning in the hearth. Three of them had stew pots sending the sweet smell of cooking pig drifting in the air.

The overseers made their rounds just after sundown; walking between the cabins and peering through the cracks in the thin planks of the walls. The four of them silently slid the iron bolts across the doors, locking them from the outside. As quiet as they were, everyone knew when they entered the Deep Corner and when they left.

I watched from the shuttered window, peeking through the spaces in the wood, as lanterns fired up one by one up on the hill. The shutters were barred just like the doors, but they could not stop me from counting the flickering lights in the big house and the overseers' cottage. When I counted ten, I jumped down from the chair. "Pappi, they are all in now."

"Are you sure?"

"Yes, sir," I said, beaming with confidence, "I used my fingers to be doubly sure of my numbers."

"All right then." Pappi lifted me back onto the chair. "Look for the faint glow of a pipe. We will wait a bit longer before we make our way."

After what seemed like half the night had passed, Pappi hoisted Isaac, my oldest brother, onto his shoulders. Isaac removed the shelf board and lifted the wall plank—its foot length—through the roof. Nate crawled through the opening in the back of the shack. He was eighteen, two years younger than Isaac and already too stocky to stand on Pappi's shoulders. This was how we escaped the shacks whenever the overseers locked us in, which wasn't all that often. Nate pulled the bar back on our door, then he and Isaac went around unlocking all the others.

I was the last to leave. I had to keep the lookout. They locked all the doors back and we left our shoes outside. If the overseer returned in the night, all would seem normal. We each wore an extra set of clothing and carried one loaf of cornbread and a hunk of meat in a handkerchief. Pappi had two hand-kerchiefs.

～

We met Cotton at the creek, past the A tree. Some of the men had torches but Cotton forbade them from lighting them. They reasoned the Peaceful was over the rise and out of sight of the creek, that traveling would be quicker and safer with at least one torch to light the way.

Cotton was adamant so he thumped Albihere, waking the faces who complained loudly to me. "Because you managed to sneak under the master's blind eye does not mean he will not come a-looking. We have the light of God and our ancestors to guide us, but we will not be safe until we pass through the Great Dismal Swamp. That is when you can feel the warmth of fire again."

He led the way, walking downstream in the creek until its black water was up to my waist. I walked beside him, my usual place, Albihere whispering warnings and guiding my steps around sharp stones and deep pockets. We exited the creek with women carrying the youngest on their backs, followed by the older children, and lastly Pappi and the other men guarding the rear. Isaac and Nate were with Pappi, being long past the age of childhood. I looked back to make sure Sara, my sister, was okay. She was carrying one of the Marcus' twins, walking between their mother and mine.

The moon was still at our back when we reached the blackness, the border of the Swamp.

Albihere said, "Horses."

For the first time, I heard all the voices speaking as one and saw through their eyes.

Pappi caught up to Cotton. "There are lights behind us. Still a good distance away."

"They ride though," Cotton said with certainty, "it will not be long before they catch up. Take a couple of men and go back a half mile and start spreading the extra food to the east. Then come back here. We will wait."

"No, you and the rest continue into the Swamp. We will catch up."

"We go as one," Albihere said to me.

"We must stick to the plan if we want to reach freedom," Cotton pointed Albihere back past the group. "The wind will carry the scent away from us and the dogs will follow. It will give us all the time we need to reach the path."

Pappi and two of the other men gave their red checkered handkerchiefs to their wives. "Aggy, I packed a little sweet bread in here for Sara and Sonny. To sweeten the sorrow if I don't make it back."

"Don't talk foolishness." Aggy stroked his face. "Now, get going, we don't have all night."

The three men ran off with their black handkerchiefs in hand. Seconds later they were lost to the darkness, and their footsteps faded even quicker.

What came next, I saw through Albihere's eyes.

Abram came to a small clearing on the path and began rolling on the ground.

The other two men looked on in bewilderment.

"Don't just stand there, help me lay down a scent track."

His two companions rolled with him through the clearing towards the east. A hundred feet in that direction they got up and ran, purposely rubbing against trees and brush as they went. They came to another clearing and the lights from the torches were visible enough to count.

"Eight torches, maybe a dozen men," Abram said. "Hear that?"

The pair nodded.

"Dogs are not far off. Let's spread the food in these bushes and get back to our families."

They headed back the way they came, again leaving their scent on the way. Before they reached the path each man broke off a Hickory branch and swept away their trail, rejoining the group when the moon was at its apex.

Pappi placed his hand on my shoulder as I sat with Cotton. "It is done. Let's get a move on."

"You men take a moment to rest," Cotton replied.

"No time. If the dogs do not pick up the false trail, they will be on us quickly."

"The dogs head east." I repeated what Albihere whispered.

Abram looked at me holding Cotton's walking stick in my lap, but I stared into the Swamp's blackness, still as a stone.

"This place holds powerful magic," Cotton whispered. "The ancestors know our plight; they guide our footsteps. It is easiest for the old ones to speak to the young ones."

"The dogs have found the bread soaked in Devil's Weed. They cannot resist its smell." My trance scared the others, but they closed in to hear my intoning. "The young ones have no sense of danger. Their parents are wiser. But they are drawn to the meats, and the White Snakeroot therein. The men and their horses have arrived."

Again, the eyes of Albihere showed me what I needed to see.

Stephen Godwin watched his tracking dogs writhing in pain. His horse dipped its head and bit into an apple on the ground beneath a bush. The other horses milled about looking and finding the treats left for them. Then the youngest of the hounds vomited a white trumpet flower amongst the half-digested bread.

Ben Skinner, the head overseer, didn't need to see anymore, "Get the horses away from here. It's a trap. The food left here is poisoned." But he was too late, as his horse collapsed under him, kicking in obvious pain. Two more horses succumbed to the poison before the rest could be pulled away. "This is a false trail. Those runaways are heading for the swamp."

"You mean the Great Dismal Swamp," Robert said. He was young, sixteen and a few months, and was on loan from the Red Mill Plantation this growing season. "I'm not going in there. My father said never to set foot on that ground. It be full of Indian spirits and other devilish things. No, sir! I am turning back right here."

"Okay." Ben took the reins of his horse. "Then you won't need your horse."

"Of course, I will!" Robert tried to pull the leather straps away, causing his steed to dance back and forth. "It is much too far to walk."

"You will not be walking," Ben drew his pistol. "I'm about to shoot you right here. And the same goes for anyone turning back." He took the boy's horse, making him walk with the others whose horses had eaten the poisoned fruit.

I held Albihere and walked alongside Cotton. I just knew where to go, although I'd never entered the Swamp. This night I'd gone as far from the plantation as I ever had. For most of my people this was as far from their homes as they had ever been too. Yet, I had no fear of the darkness that enveloped us. The crescent moon beamed a single shaft around the group. Everywhere else, blackness was but an arm's distance away.

The night had a stillness, a stifling quiet that absorbed the sound of footsteps. No insects, no hooting owls, not the sound of one's own heartbeat escaped the darkness of the Great Dismal Swamp.

Still, I saw with many eyes—mine and so many others.

"This ground is much too soft," Isaac said to Father, his voice as soft as the mud beneath his feet. "We are leaving tracks anyone can follow."

"No, we are not," Pappi answered, pointing behind them. They were no longer walking in a double line. They had bunched up in an undiscernible mass of huddled bodies. With so many feet trampling over the same ground, and the wetness of the swamp, their footprints vanished as quickly as they were formed.

"Pappi, we do not have to keep running. Nate and I and a few others can lie in wait for the slavers. Surely, we have the numbers now."

Pappi took Isaac's hand and put his other on Nate's shoulder. "May be that we outnumber our pursuers, but they have guns and whips. And we have the women and children to think about. It is best that we all survive this night."

"Survival is good," Nate said, "but not if it only leads to being hunted down and returned another night."

"Your time for fighting will be here soon enough, young Wilsons." Cotton had stopped and let the group pass him until he was side by side with Pappi and my brothers. "Our numbers grow by the night and more join each day. You speak the truth Isaac, we cannot outrun this beast, but neither can we beat it one on one."

"Who is at the lead?" Nate asked.

"Who do you think?" Cotton smiled.

"Sonny?" Nate twisted his neck to look between the bodies ahead. "But he's only twelve."

"How old do you think I was when I took the staff and walked the path to freedom?" Cotton laughed as he watched the young man trying to figure out his age. "It has been nine decades for me, seventeen fifty-four, on a night much like this. It is time for the next one to lead."

"But why Sonny?" Pappi asked but not in a questioning manner.

"Albihere chooses who it chooses. But if it comforts you, I will return to his side. Do not fall behind, we have not reached the path yet." Cotton stopped walking.

Before the three could utter another word Ol' Roy's white, cotton-topped head was at the front of the pack. He looked back and smiled.

∼

Stephen Godwin's horse whinnied and bucked at the edge of the swamp. Stephen kicked and leaned forward then patted the side of the animal's neck. "It's alright, boy, let's go."

The horse went two steps forward then back another five. He danced around in a circle, coming close to trampling those on foot.

Ben Skinner dismounted. "They will be of no use to us in there."

"See, it's like I said," Robert agreed, "the horses have better sense than to go into the Swamp. Like my daddy said—"

"Shut your mouth, boy! We can't ride in there because the ground is unfirm and the horses know they will get stuck in the mud. It has nothing to do with what foolishness your father told you. We go on foot. Now, let's hurry."

"How do you know they went this way? How do you know which way to go, Uncle Ben?" Stephen asked in a boyish tone.

"I lived my fifty years right here on this land," Ben said so all could hear, "I know every stone and stick here, and where they should be. They went this way." He pointed his torch ahead of him. But the light did not travel far into the Swamp.

∼

When Cotton and I stepped into the light of a clearing, an old Indian sat on a log. The forty with us were glad to be out of the darkness. Ahead, Cotton and the Indian shared a few words nobody understood. I looked hard at the old Indian and recognized his face but didn't know why.

As we left the clearing on the only path, Albihere spoke: "Do not stray from the path of freedom."

It was the face of the old Indian, on the walking stick, who spoke.

We all disappeared back into the darkness of the Swamp, guided by the faint light of the moon ahead, and me.

∼

A few minutes later the lights like fireflies caught the old Indian's attention.

Ben approached the man. "You be Nottuwea? I thought all your people were dead and gone from this land."

"Your kind have pushed us from our homes, but you cannot rid this land of our spirit. We are the trees, we are the rain, we are the wind."

"We are looking for our slaves. Tell me which way they went," Ben demanded.

"They follow the path to freedom." The old Indian stood. "You will not find them."

"Why not?" Stephen stepped forward from the dozen men with him.

"They follow the path to freedom. Your path leads to the darkness of your hearts."

A loud boom filled the clearing. The old Indian fell back onto the ground. A small dark red circle covered his jacketed chest. Wind blew in from every direction.

"What did you do that for!"

"He was trying to delay us, Stephen." Ben turned to the men, gun still smoking. "There is only one path out of this clearing. It's that way." He pointed his torch ahead.

"Where did the Indian go?" asked Robert.

"He ran off."

"How? You killed him!"

"Let's go!" Ben shouted, just as he would, for any questions he had no answers for. "We keep moving."

Stephen followed Ben past the log and into the darkness once more. The other men reluctantly fell behind. Robert looked at the ground one last time where the Indian had fallen and noticed there was no blood. He lagged behind the group.

The men held two torches together to brighten the flame. But the light shone no farther; they could see a yard ahead and no more. The solid ground showed no footprints; it was smooth and undisturbed.

Stephen spoke up. "Are we sure we're on the right path?"

One of the overseers stumbled and left the small circle of light. He screamed.

The others turned to see him up to his thighs in black ooze. Two men stepped forward, reached their hands to pull him out. But other hands reached up his legs and pulled him down deeper. He screamed for help, but his friends retreated in fear.

"It is quicksand, boys," Ben warned. "Step back or it will pull you in too." Meanwhile, the black hands pulled the man under. "Let's go," he continued. "And watch your step, they don't call this place the Great Dismal Swamp without reason."

Robert lingered longer, as if his fears had been confirmed.

The rest went only a few more yards, only a few minutes, when a loud roar broke through the silence. A dark mass barreled into the group. In a flash, one man's midsection was ripped from his body, and another was carried off. Two others fired their rifles into the blackness.

Robert, frozen, stared at the man's severed body.

"*Bear*," Ben hissed. "*Bears!* Let's go. Those slaves are getting away."

He quickened his gait, causing the others to do the same.

Robert picked up the torch that had been carried by the man who disappeared into the Swamp and waited a few seconds before following. "No safety in numbers," he whispered to the night. "Not here."

A swarm of mosquitoes was drawn to the light of the torches. The men swung their flames wildly trying to fend them off. Robert watched as black lines traced the veins of the men who were stung. Their faces swelled quickly and they fell.

Ben, moving fast, too fast not to show his panic, set fire to the five dead men. It drew the bugs away from him. Suddenly, he eyed Robert hanging back and drew his pistol.

Robert saw it just in time and tossed his torch onto the heap of burning flesh. Then he disappeared into the darkness, running full out as shots like dull drumbeats sounded. He could not see where he was going but the ground beneath his feet was solid, so he kept going.

Stephen, off from the others, heard the growl of wolves, the war cries of Indians, and a thousand angry voices. He could not see his Uncle Ben. Or any of the others. They'd been swept away by the blackness, plucked out of existence, there was no other way to describe it.

Out of nowhere a faint glowing figure approached.

Stephen drew his pistol with shaking hands. "Who are you? What do you want from me?"

"Freedom," I said, hearing myself speak through the lips of Albihere's faces. "It is all we ever wanted."

"I was good to you. Not like my father. I played games with you."

"You wanted to play with me, you had no one else to play

with." I stood inches from him, but my voice sounded like we stood across a field. "I had to play with you. I had no choice."

"Don't you think I wish I could be free? Not have to look after you. I didn't want this."

"You can walk away, anytime you like. We have to run."

I paused.

We paused.

"But don't take too long," we said. "Your chance for freedom is fading. And we will be back to take ours."

I left, fading from Stephen's view, but we watched for a long time while he stumbled in the darkness.

THE END

THE RAINMAKER

I NTERNATIONAL ATMOSPHERIC PRESSURE & TEMPERATURE CONTROL SATELLITE: (I.A.P.T.C.S.) REPORTING: 12:00 AM Dec. 14, 1990, 150o.42'15"W. by 60o.N.

The teletype at the arctic tracking center began receiving its weather data. A blue dot appeared in the lower quarter of the radar screen; the dot represented the 8-ton fusion-powered civilian satellite; her orbit was tracking 100. She was right on target on her 40,000th trip around the globe.

Her message was transmitted in a tenth of a second as IAPTCS disappeared for another six hours. Patrick Molloy tore a colorful map from the teletype, IAPTCS had broken up a high-pressure block over the Nebraskans, decreased humidity in South America and gave a 2-degree shift to a threatening electrical storm in the Pacific. She was very busy, on this one of her six-hour long flight paths, two hundred miles above the Earth.

General Wood of N.A.R.C. (North America Radar Command) ripped his sheet from the printer; his tracking board had the satellite moving 18 degrees east over the U.S.S.R. mainland. The report was identical to the one in Molloy's possession, except the last line. 'Hot spot surface level… varying position.'

Gen. Wood picked up the telephone, "Sargeant, bring me the updates from the Mark Six." A hot spot meant some kind of engine was being operated, varying position only spelt one thing to the general, a convoy. If it was a convoy, the spy satellite known as Mark Six would have a good picture. The general poured himself a little coffee and cleaned his desk.

In came a stocky, well-suited gentleman with a manila envelope in hand. "These pics were transmitted five minutes ago," informed the red-haired sergeant, "the Russians are sending a lot of guys on hikes these days."

Gen. Wood pulled the photos out and spread them on the desk. One picture, a high-speed closeup, caught his attention immediately. Three flatbed tractors and a tanker were detailed clearly in the eight by ten glossy. "Perhaps the hikes weren't just for exercise."

The general gave the sergeant a salute, dismissing him. He knew a rocket when he saw one, even on three different trucks. The telemetry at the bottom of the photograph placed them well within the U.S.S.R. Gen. Wood drank a bit from his mug and began strolling his office. Circling an oblong florescent-topped table he flicked a switch, and a map appeared. He took his red chalk marking stick and drew a bold 'X' where the convoy was positioned. He continued around until he came to the control console again. He pushed a couple of yellow buttons on the lower row, changing the map almost unnoticeably.

If the Russ built a missile site it should show in the time delay photograph, thought the general. Yet, he saw nothing. He depressed a green panel and the map zoomed closer. Still nothing. Another panel, another map, another blank. Perhaps they were not intending to install the goose but merely transporting it. Gen. Wood went over to his desk and called for a meeting at 0200. He ordered a recon to leave the aircraft carrier Manhattan immediately. Destination, forty thousand feet above and slightly east of the Kolyma Mountains. Troop movements could be ignored sometimes, however, S.A.C. Intelligence (Strategic Air Command) never let artillery go unchecked.

Capt. Greenfur received his orders on board the Manhattan stationed in the North Atlantic. Within minutes he was off in a supersonic spy plane called the Hummingbird.

The sky was a clear light-blue over the arctic. IAPTCS said the weather should be perfect for low altitude shoots over the U.S.S.R. Capt. Greenfur checked his position and began rolling the cameras. His orders read, 'a missile or transporter should be out on the tundra.' There wasn't a Russian ship in the area, the Manhattan had already confirmed that fact. The pilot watched his viewscreen carefully for a hanger or silo door in the frozen wasteland.

He was jetting towards the northern slopes of the Kolyma range when he spotted a building close to its base. Just a small aluminum shack about fifty feet long. It wasn't big enough to be a hanger, but Greenfur thought its location warranted pictures. He snapped a couple with his high-speed nose camera.

Capt. Greenfur's ears split when the radar warning suddenly screamed. Three Migs appeared on the scope, each coming from a different direction. Greenfur took his only option, he pulled back hard on his throttle with his right hand and equally as hard on the joystick in his left. The Hummingbird shot up and out of range without incident. Its radio facsimile was already being received at the North American Radar Center.

Gen. Wood, Gen. Lesser, and Com. Westly were gathered at the center's command post. Around the room pictures flashed on the overheads. The center was a beehive of activity. Lines to the pentagon were bussing as the high command joined the all-out alert. Twelve other radar centers fed data to N.A.R.C. Command Post from around the world to be analyzed. One of

Greenfur's pictures that appeared on the overheads, the building jutting out of the mountain, detailed a fresh roadbed.

"That's what we are looking for," Gen. Lesser said, "the door to the Russian's newest silo."

"Yes! That's the entrance alright, but I can't find the hole in these pics," agreed Com. Westly. "Maybe the Ruskies have yet to complete the launch facilities."

Gen. Wood walked over to the electronic mapping table, a green light marked the building's position, and a red light signaled the last reported site of the convoy. He motioned to the others, "You better believe it's completed. That hot spot is about a hundred miles from that base. They wouldn't risk detection if it wasn't operational."

"That's true. Wherever the hole is you can bet your last buck it's pointing right at us!"

"Les is right," Wood continued, "the Russians have had some trouble with open air test fires in the north sector. With unpredictable weather conditions and all, a permanent under-ground site makes sense. The only question is, how big is the goose they intend to install?"

Com. Westly looked at him earnestly, "And when do they intend to use it. They never tried to put a silo this far north before. If they planned an over-the-top attack, it was always thought it would be a bomber run. This changes our defense package dramatically."

The three men studied the collage of information provided by the vast network of high technology. A red phone lit up on the communication desk.

Gen. Wood answered it. After a few minutes of 'Yes, sir' he rejoined the two officers. "Well, Washington wants confirmation."

"Confirmation! Jesus Christ, what do they want, a fireball over Michigan?"

"They want a clear shot of that missile assembly or silo

opening or something positive," returned Wood, "before they start screaming foul."

"We have about a hundred miles before that hot spot disappears into the mountain. And close to two days before it is operational," Com. Westly said.

"We can't get someone into the area undetected. Not at such short notice. Once operational, a shot from there would be nearly impossible to intercept," commented Gen. Lesser.

The lanky, gray-haired Gen. Wood, called the Scrambler by his friends in the forces, pulled a report from the desk. He handed the paper to Gen. Lesser; it was IAPTCS latest weather conditions. "Maybe we can stop the convoy before it gets there. Or even close down that base for good."

"We can't strike that deep in Soviet territory without starting something," Com. Westly said, fearing a wild plan from the Scrambler.

"We don't have to strike. We can let nature do the work with our help. The reason the Russ have never planted a base this far north is that it is practically useless due to bad weather. With the new technologies and a powerful booster to give it a good liftoff, they can overcome the weather " Gen. Wood's eyes were dark, set deep in his hardened face. They peered at the other two in the soft light of the map table. They looked dead; lifeless pools where many souls had drowned. "IAPTCS is on her northern swing over the Atlantic. It will pass a developing storm center. Instead of breaking it up, suppose we strengthen it. Build it into a real killer, then hurtle her right at those Russians. We can bog down that convoy, perhaps bury the base for good."

The three men agreed it was a good plan. One hell of a good plan. If timed right, they could get somebody in behind the blizzard to examine the rocket. The computers went to work on the details. Gen. Wood ordered a line opened to the satellite's control. High priority. Coded.

IAPTCS crossed the equator on schedule. Its onboard inertial guidance computer system switched into active mode. The starboard retro-engine fired a five second blast slowing the hourglass-shaped satellite to twenty thousand miles per minute. Thus, rolling its eight-ton body off her preset path.

In the aft compartment another computer worked on its new directives. The bathtub-sized fusion generator, the heart of IAPTCS located in the neck, stepped up power forty percent. From the tail, a broad thick paddle dotted with glowing cylinders produced a high magnetic charge. Another door slid open on the satellite and infrared beams poured out.

The Athena, a cruise ship in the Caribbean seas was having a marvelous first day out. Life bubbled on her decks under cloudless skies and easy breezes.

A fishing schooner called it an early day, pulling in half full nets. The captain remarked to his first mate, "Fish are running opposite to the sea. That's a sure sign to set your sails by mate." The patchwork of gray and blue stretched out of sight. While gulls raced with the wind towards the New England coast.

The Manhattan released a high-altitude weather balloon. It tugged violently at its hold lines. Bolts of bright blue lightning crackled across the clouds rugged underbellies. IAPTCS zipped overhead two hundred miles down range.

Once past the arctic, the satellite's internal computer corrected the longitude tracking. Fusion step-down began.

An altitude tracking error was detected. IAPTCS fired her single booster rocket. The two million or so circuits-brain registered a major orbital quake. It tumbled end on end twice. Then, for the first time in the International Atmospheric Control Program's five-year history IAPTCS went silent.

Worldwide pandemonium spread through the radio-wave saturated air. Military and civil radar stations broke into chaos over the thought of the eight-ton fusion projectile going amok. Jets ripped away from nearly three hundred sites around the globe. Top priority, to find and track. In Michigan the order was received by Gen. Wood of N.A.R.C., less than a half hour after he sent the spacecraft its first military assignment.

His staff were hot on the case, feeding their computers data on the sat's changes in orbit and energy expenditures. The computer's tapes spun, and lights flashed as the mechanical brains tried to figure out what had happened onboard the satellite. On the main tracking board, a broad green line traced its way across the pictured continents.

The line represented a fifty-mile span that the computers suggested the satellite would travel along. Gen. Wood relayed the message to Washington with circumstances of the past hour. He also suggested the satellite be destroyed, for security reasons.

By two A.M. the news spanned the entire world. Reporters descended on the White House by the scores. In the capitals of the other member nations, who helped build and finance the weather machine, an angry and frightened populace raged. The one question on everyone's lips, "Is the satellite coming down hot?"

By 2:05 A.M. December 14 the President of the United States appeared before the TV cameras in the East Wing "After contacting other leaders, it has been agreed, the satellite will be detonated before it has a chance to re-enter the atmosphere. The risk to human life is minimum, but it will not be taken lightly. At present there is no reason for alarm."

A reporter from the L.A. Times jumped to his feet, "Isn't it true the satellite is equipped with a powerful nuclear generator?"

"The satellite should eject the fusion power supply into deep space automatically when its orbit starts to decay. But we lost communication with IAPTCS, so we thought it wise to destroy her, as an added precaution."

"N.Y. Post here, Mr. President," a stout Black man in hornrims took the opportunity to cut in, "how did the satellite lose control? And are there any backup systems to regain control of it?"

"At this time, I do not have an answer to your first question. And yes, there are backup systems to the craft's guidance control. But without some kind of signal from the craft, we must assume they are inoperative. At this time, we have the most sophisticated planes from all the major countries trying to locate and determine the satellite's condition. I'm sorry, gentlemen, but that is the extent of what we know now. I'll be briefing you the moment something develops."

"Suppose it is already down," shouted the same man as the president started to leave.

"Impossible!" Shouted back the weary man from the doorway.

Pat Malloy had received word of the mishap like everyone else. He intently watched his screen. 'All present and accounted for', he noted in the log. Snow fell heavily outside the installation. Very heavy. Too heavy, he thought. Pat glanced back over the weather report he received two hours earlier. Strange, no word of a major storm. He pondered. "She must have really blown a fuse up there to be this wrong," he commented to the empty room. Suddenly, there was a blinding flash in the western sky. Thunder rocked the lonely outpost. Patrick hit the window in time to see a blueish comet streak past.

Six men rushed into the room.

"I think we just located IAPTCS."

Ken Brooks was at the radarscope's control, "There's nothing on the screen. And I can't pick it up on the remote units either."

"Impossible," Patrick retorted," that sat just passed overhead no more than fifteen miles up. I'm sure of that!"

"No matter, I'm reporting in just the same," Sam Collin told the group.

The report was received and confirmed by several other S.A.C. stations. An interceptor was at that minute racing to cut off the runaway. The sat was skipping along the earth's atmosphere a hundred miles out of the green band on N.A.R.C.'s screens.

From the cockpit of Capt. Botley's jet, he saw the fusion-propelled missile changing direction randomly. He swung in behind the sat and flipped a lever on the dashboard. Two red words appeared on the panel, "Rockets Ready". He watched the range meter... 10 miles... 20 miles... 30 miles. When the satellite was sixty miles ahead of him and seemingly holding steady, his thumb eased down on the firing button of the joystick. Two reddish white clouds streamed out in front of him. Capt. Batley dove out of the sky, "Rockets away and locked on target. Impact in 6...5...4 ...3..."

Two immense explosions lit up the twilight above him. His craft shook hard, but he held control. Too soon he thought. "Bogey's alive!" Capt. Batley reported and started his ship climbing.

A Japanese carrier confirmed the report with sonic tracking devices. The satellite was not only intact but within the earth's atmospheric blanket now. All reports drew the same conclusion, IAPTCS would not make another orbit.

Gen. Wood watched his board with IAPTCS's position correctly marked over the Pacific. With any luck, he thought, the eight-ton monster would tumble harmlessly into the ocean. But luck was not blowing the general's way. IAPTCS passed over the Pacific

Ocean, over the Indian Ocean and smashed into the frozen icepack of Antarctica.

The world held its breath, waiting for the mushroom cloud that would tell if it hit, fusion generator and all. A U.S. bomber trailed the craft by only five minutes. The crew was expecting to pass right through the center of the blast. Instead, they flew smoothly over with automatic cameras snapping away. They circled, dropping dye bombs, marking a perimeter on the ice. On the next time around, paratroopers leaped onto the quiet scene. The pilot released the contamination equipment and flew eastward, reporting all secured.

Gen. Wood sighed at first, then ordered an update on the arctic circle conditions. It was described in two words, "blinding blizzard."

Com. Westly had his newly formed Bear Unit on alert. The turbine tractor was as large as a semi. Nicknamed Snowball, the vehicle held twenty men, a vast assortment of machine guns, cannons, rockets, and a laser guidance system which meant uninhibited driving. He ordered the team into Soviet territory to intercept the convoy and tagged the message, "No Capture". A suicide mission. For a moment, Com. Westly wished he was heading the assignment. The massive machine plowed through the dense white wall at fifteen miles an hour. Com. Westly rejoined his two comrades in the command post. He placed a hand on each man's shoulder, "They'll have confirmation soon."

"Les got to the sixth fleet and they are on top of the situation down there," said Gen. Wood. His eyes fixed on the long board, as it was popularly called. He began in a low tone, "We have a lot riding here, boys. Washington is between a sword and a gun. There will be flakes flying in every direction. Just about every nation is going to want in."

"Stanton is good. He'll hold a hundred miles." Westly was being optimistic. He knew the fight would be waged in the capital.

"This thing must be handled fast. We have to get to that satellite and secure its condition!"

Lesser's condition was the PM 700 Computer. Inside its five individual memory banks lay the commands to change course. Along with orders directly conversed to its prime function. One of the banks was shielded, in case of meltdown, it contained the internal-external telemetric memory. The bank, a heavy leaded shoe box, formed the main junction between IAPTCS's twelve computers. This would be what the war was all about. Who would retrieve this flight log from its icepack grave.

"Bruce Wells," blurted out Gen. Wood.

Lesser made a half-hearted plea to go strictly Airforce personnel. Finally, he stated, "Wells walked out on us at JPL."

Out of the darkness explosions repeated rhythmically. Suddenly, and with catlike precision, she was running down the narrowing garden paths. Obstructions blocked his view, slowed his pursuit. Thunder continued ripping apart the forest, revealing the blackness. Another round of heavy thuds was followed instantly by a brittle crackle. Bruce sprang to his feet confused and sleepy. Blinding light painfully filled his bedroom. His hands raced to his eyes, burglars or terrorists, he thought.

"Mr. Wells. Sorry about the intrusion," a concerned but unsympathetic voice acknowledged.

Bruce recognized the uniform of Airforce security, but not the face under its blue on white cap.

To the four officers, Bruce Wells appeared understandably shocked. His five-eight body shaking from unconscious fear. His red eyes darting about in their sockets.

Bruce tried to muster strength in his words, "what the hell is this? What the fuck do you want?"

One of the airmen snapped forward handing the young man his I.D.

Bruce looked it over carefully, he had seen them thousands of times, at hundreds of airbases. Finally, he said, "So, I'm too old to draft… I hope."

"We have orders to take you to Antarctica, immediately." Responded the man cold and hard.

A second man spoke up, "Surely you've heard IAPTCS is down."

Bruce wasn't too sure he wasn't still dreaming, like the jungle girl. Perhaps this was a kidnapping plot. He had to verify this news. Instinctively Bruce looked to his left arm for the time, then to the night table's clock. "Jesus! It's near four in the morning."

"Yes, sir, I apologize again… but time is essential."

"I'll have to confirm what you said." Bruce turned on a large black radio, flipped a few switches, turned one of many knobs and waited. Nothing. He turned more knobs, pushed buttons, threw switches.

The announcer rang out, "The big story for this hour on all news radios. Nuclear powered satellite crashes. Bruce Wells, designer of the weather control satellite is said to be enroute to the site…"

Bruce snapped off the system, "I'll just be a minute or two dressing."

The third officer handed him a medium-sized tote bag. "Everything you'll need for now, sir. We have a chopper on the roof, so just grab your coat, time is really short."

The 'Everything you need' brought back vivid memories of military security. The sort that didn't let you bring your own toothbrush. It was the base of the conflicts that led him to quit the Jet Propulsion Laboratory, right after the IAPTCS project was up. "Fine job you guys did on the door," Bruce commented climbing over half of it.

"Don't worry, my two men will stand guard until the Air Force sends someone to take care of it."

The helicopter ride was too short for Bruce to find out who had sent for him. Security men were pretty tight-lipped. Long enough, though, for him to dress in thermal and poly-quilts, for the extreme cold. He checked and found one tooth-brush in his coat pocket, he fished for a device which resembled a pocket camera. He carefully slipped it into his waistband, while the officers carefully evaded his queries.

Bruce was quickly shuttled to an awaiting supersonic transport. A set of papers were shoved into his hands marked, 'TOP SECRET: MR. BRUCE WELLS'. On board he was directed to the rear by a blonde trying hard not to look military in her civies.

"At ease!" He commanded snidely.

In the pastel green lounge deep in their chairs, two women were having coffee and sandwiches. Of the seven people, Bruce knew two, Dr. Kass by reputation and Nancy Turner much better.

As he crossed the lounge towards her, a giant red face intercepted, "Mr. Wells, glad you could make our party. I'm Com. Thomas, I'll be the top man at the site."

"Looks like it's been a rough night for you. Just like me," Nancy handed him a coffee.

The plane started off, and lights passed as a steady yellow line. Bruce concluded only three others as regulars. The rest were sharp-cut military personnel. As he dropped into the chair next to Nancy's the commander went into his act. Thomas gave a quick synopsis of what had happened, with some facts omitted, and what was going on at the moment.

Bruce found himself sleeping comfortably on Nancy's shoulder. She slept with one hand tightly gripping his thigh. Nervousness, anxiety, and foreboding brought consciousness to Bruce Wells. His neck stiffened as he stirred in the soft cushion. Nancy's hand slid across his leg into his foggy sight. A whispered sweet moan filled his left ear. Nancy rolled sideways in her reclined bucket seat, then back again. Her vision cleared to Bruce's face. He was smiling, like you see in a faded picture. Her chestnut eyes were surrounded by a wild forest of Redwoods.

"Good morning," someone finally said. It was Com. Thomas.

The two Airforce stewardesses were busy in the kitchen. Fresh maps, pictures, and coffee had been laid out. Something odd indeed caught Bruce's attention on his way to use his government issues. He picked up a copy of the New York Times, today's copy. He, of course, was front page news. Here we go again, he thought, but who the hell went out for a paper?

"Radio print," offered Com. Thomas. He was a robust man. Regular army, as they say, but with a warm countenance. That was probably why he was Airforce, Bruce mused. When his first statement didn't draw a reply, the commander went on the offensive. "Look, I know your history. You don't like the military, and I mean all of it, me included. That's fine. Everyone's entitled, but we have got a job to do... and a lot is hanging on us working as a team. So, are you with me, I mean all the way down the line?"

"If you answer one question?"

"From the top," Com. Thomas said frankly.

"Whose team is this? Who picked me?"

"General Wood."

Hot damn, Bruce thought, looking at his tired face in the mirror. Gen. Wood was one of the top-brass who had wanted him ousted. When they had wanted a restricted bank installed for NATO members only, Bruce protested strongly. Finally, they had settled for a few override functions and some restricted transmissions. National security had been maintained. Now, he knew somebody had screwed up big. He glanced out the window, seven glimmering beer cans floated below. Ahead, the ice pack, Antarctica.

Back in the lounge another update was in progress. Com. Thomas was giving Mr. Jensen and Dr. Macotti final instructions on news releases. They were the pressmen of this team. When introduced to them six hours ago, Bruce tagged the two as Yes Men.

Nancy had changed clothes and was attending to Dr. Kass. Bruce swooped up his unopened top secrets, ripped the top from it and started half-heartedly leafing through the pages. He looked directly into Kass' steel-grey eyes, "You know I wrote most of the stuff here."

Kass replied in an easy but careful manner, "Yes, I know your rep, as they say, outshines you. There have been some changes since you were with the project. I'm really pleased to be working with you, only, I wish the situation was a little more relaxed."

"More preliminary tests were performed," Nancy injected, "looks like the reactor is active."

"Well, looks like this is going to be a fun day," Bruce tried to lift her spirits, but only managed to sound sarcastic. He walked away quietly to get a cup of coffee he didn't want.

As the minutes passed, he read the papers and sipped steaming hot coffee. Dr. Kass approached with cup in hand. "Bruce, it is you who has to go down there to access the problem, and I know how you feel about the mainstream, but we're not trying to put one over on anybody. Now, you better do your homework, we go to work in a half hour."

Gen. Wood received a coded message from Snowball: Travel

very difficult. Visibility almost zero. Most likely to pass objective without knowing. Relay any supportive info.

He would have sent a reply if he had one. The blizzard was so thick even their best equipment was worthless. Snowball was on its own, he only hoped they could get something concrete on the Russians. Things were heating up over IAPTCS's crash world round. The crater was expanding and filling with water. Rumors had the satellite opened on impact and spilling atomic material into the highly receptive ice. Sonar images verified that the satellite came down fully intact, yet the stories persisted.

The tower of steam was Bruce's first view. Then the red markings on the ice for the airstrip. On the approach, he was able to pick out the tents of the makeshift camp. Just before touchdown, while he was suiting up, he eyed the crater. A smooth circular aperture that grew smaller as it got deeper, until there was only a stormy sea of clouds shooting forth its pale ivory monolith. Bruce thought of the Tower of Bable when he was speaking to Mr. Jensen, supposedly, a Belgian physicist sent by the overseas investors.

The skis of the supersonic jet touched lightly on the frigid surface. They sped past the hole almost instantaneously, arced widely and came to a stop a few feet from its edge. Bruce whispered to Nancy, "Now that's door-to-door service."

They exited the craft, hurrying to the tents. It was amazingly warm. Not much of a wind either, Bruce noticed. From the shelter of the monitoring tent, they watched the jet take off. In its wake stood a monstrous crane supporting an oblong diving bell. This is what they broke into his house and dragged him around the globe for, to take a steam bath in Antarctica. "Boy, don't I feel crazy," Bruce let slip.

"Don't let it scare you," Com Thomas reaffirmed, "it has

been down a hundred times already. As I told you, one of our engineers will go down with you the first time."

A man placed his hand on Bruce's shoulder, "Ken Baggis." Bruce turned to face the man, Ken was slightly less than average height, dark glasses and a permanent smile. "I am taking you down. I admit I haven't gone all the way, but I will if you want some backup. I guess I'm the expert in Bella."

"No, I think I'll get it together. No sense in risking both of our heads. Time comes… Everyone pulls back."

"You'll see."

It wasn't long before Bruce saw. He walked out on the ramp that led from the crane house to the bell. As he walked across the abyss, a large slab of ice abruptly tore away from the wall and slid out of sight in the cloud below.

"That type of action is going on all the time. When I first arrived, the crater was thirty feet wide, now it's close to forty and it has been less than eight hours."

"That's really interesting," Bruce noted. "How long before the crane falls in?"

"Maybe by tomorrow it will be useless to us." The two men climbed through the side hatch of Bella. "The arm can be extended," continued Ken from inside, "but after tomorrow, we won't be able to reach the center anymore. Come over here, let me give you the rundown. The whole system can be operated from inside the bell."

Ken buckled himself into one of the seats up on the control deck. Bruce was at the forward access hatch with his back to Ken, he slipped the pocket camera-like device into the bay. Bruce bounced up the ladder to the control deck. Ken looked at him oddly while he got ready in the chair.

"How far down have you gone in this thing?" Bruce tried to play off the inquisitive look.

"Just to the base of the crater, I stopped at the opening to the subterranean fissure IAPTCS is creating. My job is to take pictures, and that's it. Buddy Boy, I can do that from a distance without disengaging the hookup." Ken began lowering the bell by pushing on the right pedal.

Bruce switched on the flood lights, cameras, and the radios. "This is it!" He exclaimed to the goosenecked mike.

"Good Luck," responded Nancy instantly from the overhead speaker.

Luck, thought Bruce. Somehow that didn't sound important. Another hunk of ice sheared off the wall, a resounding crackle penetrating the minisub.

Ken was describing the operations of Bella's hand levers which controlled the front grapplers. There was another set of levers between the men which controlled Bella's motion when she was in the subterranean sea.

Bella reached the knotted cloud at the base of the crater. Bruce read the gauges, one read, 'minus eighty feet.' The craft shook and trembled as she entered the turbulence. The single viewscreen was a hazy, shapeless red and green mess. Thick black lines traversed its illuminous face. "This answers some of my questions," Bruce pointed to one of the black bands. "The sonic and infrared images show no patterns. That is normal, but the magnetic sensor is registering an increasing pull."

"So, what does that tell you?" It was Dr. Kass.

Bruce looked to the microphone, "IAPTCS must be trying to control its external environment."

"Why would it do that? She already crashed," Ken said lowering them steadily.

"Maybe IAPTCS doesn't know it is down," offered Bruce, only half believing his own words. After all, with her array of radio altimeters the sat could measure distance to an eighth of an inch, so how could she not know. His eyes caught a glimpse of jagged ice, which was the beginning of the impact area. It was hard for him to accept that IAPTCS had made an eighty-foot depression before it even hit. Perhaps the sat had come down backward. Its main booster could have melted the ice, no, he dispelled the idea, there would be a lake in the ice. Instead, he was in a crater. It didn't make any sense.

The tunnel ended, fanning out into a bubbling sea and high ceiling cave. Ken interrupted his ponderings, "This is as far as I have gone."

Bruce reached up and pulled a red ring, "Well, you are going to get your first close-up look." The bell splashed down into the steaming water.

Both men grabbed their levers tightly against the whirlpool tide. Above their heads, through the portal, danced random lightning bolts. Always in front of them, hovering over the dark motionless center, IAPTCS.

Streaking around in Bella, all twenty-six feet of her top-hatted barracuda body, Bruce called out, "So this is probably what a black hole looks like to IAPTCS. What a place to build one."

"I didn't want to see what IAPTCS looked like," cried out Ken Baggis. He worked his set of four directional levers frantically. He looked at Bruce sitting quietly. "Anytime you think it's good to make a move." Then he looked at IAPTCS.

She sat plowing yellowish behind a red haze. Her thirty feet of glazed steel never came closer, never farther. Her hourglass bells held rows of dark metal, running her outer perimeters a row of tiny lights. The inside rings had two panels on each end of the generator. Bella flowed endlessly around IAPTCS. Ken relaxed his grasp.

"If we can get closer to the edge without getting crushed by the immense magnetic field, we might get IAPTCS under control."

"You're the expert," Ken was giving him that look again, "I'm glad you know what's going on."

"Oh! I don't know what's happening here." Bruce was

watching him for the first time. "I do want to find out though, at first sign of trouble, we hit the A.R.S."

"Shit, I was going to hit that button when you pulled the release cord, Bruce." Ken nudged the forward throttle.

Bella slowly pulled away from the satellite.

"What's happening now, Bruce!"

"We're moving backwards."

"I see that! Time to push…"

"Not yet," Bruce spun to the other end of the control deck. "Let me try reversing the polarity."

"That's your problem, you don't know when you're in trouble. Do you?"

"I've been in trouble since two this morning. I'd kinda like to get out soon. There we go." Bruce made a few jerking motions back to his seat. They were still spinning, drawing in on her. The ship's nose spread extending slinky metal arms.

"Easy, be real slow, just a little at a time."

"Ken, this would be easier if you didn't talk about it." Bruce operated three of the six arms; Bella revolved slowly as she approached.

Ken manipulated the throttles smoothly. "It is calming down," he informed.

"I expected it to," Bruce boosted. He pushed forward on a lever and an arm reacted accordingly. He watched the dial in front of him.

Ken stared at the flickering needles at his station. "Is everything O.K. so far?"

"Not too bad. No spill over at least."

Ken had heard that before in the navy, with the submarine crew of Orca, an atomic. The boys used the term to describe engine room leaks. Another arm extended like an antenna on a fish. This one held a black object on its end. Bruce's device reached out to the wide end of IAPTCS. It stopped a mere foot from the flashing lights. Bruce clicked a few more circuits to life, and gently placed the object on the satellite. To Ken's amazement it remained when the arm retracted.

"Back us up slowly," Bruce said.

Ken pulled back on the middle throttle.

Bruce dropped lightly down the ladder. He reached a bank of computers that was in a kaleidoscopic frenzy. A few hits at the soft board and he settled them down. He went back to the control deck. "Good. This is good enough. I placed an override access system on the sat's auxiliary command station. We are receiving data now."

Ken watched the satellite all the while. It was a dizzying experience. Bruce went to work at the bridge computer. Ken whirled around in his chair to watch the computer's lights go on as the memory filled. Not that he understood much of it. He glanced at Bruce; he was absorbed by the changing images on the computer's monitor. Finally, nervousness set in, "Can we get the hell out of here?"

"Oh, sure, yeah, a few more minutes," Bruce was jolted by the harshness of his tone. "I am nearly finished collecting IAPTCS's internal report. I am going to try transmitting to the surface now, you know we lost contact after separation. From what I have seen, IAPTCS has got her brains fried."

Seconds later a barrage of voices echoed in the sub.

The most notable was Com. Thomas, "What the Jackshit are you two doing down there? Ken... Bruce Walls respond if you can... Somebody get me their down time."

"I got us reception," stated Bruce.

"I think the chief is in a panic," chuckled Ken, "there goes his pension."

Bruce spoke into his mike, "We're fine and coming up. Do you copy?"

"Copy this..."

Bruce snapped off the receiver on Com. Thomas. "They are reading us."

The commander was at the safe line as Bella reached the berth. His face was bleeding red, streaked by sweat.

Nancy pushed past him out onto the ramp. She met the pair with a furious outburst, "how could you, Ken? Bruce doesn't know how to control her yet. You both might have been killed. This was supposed to be a practice run."

"I tried to persuade this joker," Ken's eyes conveyed his true feelings to Bruce. "I think she's stuck on you."

"Real schoolboy," Nancy calmly stated, "you are supposed to be working with us. And by the book. No surprises, Bruce."

As the trio passed by Com. Thomas he softly said, "Full report, Ken." Minutes later, he was in Bruce's tent. Nancy excused herself politely, leaving the two men to battle it out. "Look, Wells, I'm going to pull you off of this assignment. I can't afford to keep on anyone who's not totally with us."

"O.K. I should have informed you that I was going all the way in." Bruce took a chance, he knew from the commander's look at the ramp, this was about the access system he had used, non-issue.

"Damn that!" Com. Thomas exploded, "You are transmitting data on a nonregulation line. I've been trying to jam it out. I want you to stop that carrier signal… Or I want you out."

Nancy entered after the commander marched out. Before she could begin, Bruce spoke, "I'm not going anywhere, Nan. He needs me. I think more than he knows. Go review IAPTCS's internal data and match it to her output generators. I need to know what you think. I'll be going over some prelims until lunch."

As Nancy passed the command tent, Ken was there, giving what looked like a colorful report. She hurried along the few yards of helicopter pads to the communication tent. Inside, Dr. Kass was at the computer keyboard. A CRT flickering its information in a myriad of charts, numbers, and graphs. Nancy sat next to the aging doctor. "He said to compare the internal sensors to the sat's output operations."

"Many of the functions are gone. Wiped out," he stated. Nancy didn't respond. The doctor turned to face her, his tone sharp. "The satellite is running without any controls. Its onboard computer must have suffered severe damage on impact. Many of the override functions are down, there are only sketchy internal reports being transmitted. I do not know if we can trust the data we're receiving from it."

"If we correlate the outside conditions with what we are receiving maybe we will get a clearer picture of her situation," Nancy injected a little note of hope into the statement.

"Without a full report on the fusion reactor and its fuel supply, we're sitting on a time bomb." Dr. Kass was blunt.

Nancy knew it was because of Bruce. Perhaps his way of warning her not to let a romantic past cloud her professional judgement. She quietly took a position at a CRT to study the information.

Lunch was anything but quiet. Shouting matches broke out among Bruce, Dr. Kass, and the commander. Each strongly opposed to the others' plan for handling IAPTCS.

Dr. Kass proposed severing the output option computer, which would automatically shut down the reactor. Bruce pointed out that the fuel feeder could be damaged, and the reactor would overload. If this was true, a huge plasmic cloud would be released, consuming all matter it contacted.

Com. Thomas wanted to drain the fuel tanks and remove the magnetic bubble, causing a subatomic explosion. Both Dr. Kass and Bruce were opposed to this solution. They feared the explosion, even non-nuclear, would be devasting.

As Bruce put it, "Huge chunks of ice will be thrown thousands of miles away to strike like missiles. Maybe two or three tons each." But he was the one who came up with an alternative procedure. He agreed that the fuel supply would have to be dumped. Then the reactor would be flooded with nitrogenated water, the satellite might be recovered. The problem was time. Time to drain the tanks, to mix the water and nitrogen, and the major task of feeding it to the reactor.

The only thing they all agreed on was that time was running out fast. Bruce knew he had to go down that night. The cavern was spreading at an accelerating rate. His studies turned up one definite conclusion. He waited for the others to run out of wind. Then he stated, "In about twelve hours IAPTCS will have created an environment of volcanism." His words had no room for debate. "At that time IAPTCS may launch itself back into space."

Everyone stopped eating; the sound of forks and knives clanking to rest in tin plates as everyone digested the thought.

Nancy cleared her throat, "You think the satellite will hit the land mass by then?"

"No. But it will have built up enough force to blast a steam ball into the atmosphere. I'm not sure IAPTCS can survive. The generator could rupture anytime. Anytime. I know the ice pack cannot hold the pressure more than another twelve hours. It could flash atomic. We could end up with a hell of a tornado ravishing the earth. It could melt the ice pack completely. We could have a flood of biblical proportions. I am talking Noah's Ark destruction."

Com. Thomas stretched across the table with a clenched fist-pound in his words, "We have to make a control detonation as soon as possible. We can try a two-fisted approach. Ignite the sat's fuel supply and contain that with a surface level blast."

Dr. Kass quickly agreed. He pointed out a large spread for the second explosion, an extremely potent one, would ensure containment to a small area. The cleanup would then be easy. The two men left to map out the details, as a secondary option.

"Nan, why do I feel like this whole party is a seek and destroy mission?"

"It is." Nancy Turner responded coldly. He could feel the intensity in her voice. Her eyes were a steadfast indictment.

"What's wrong with trying to save her."

"Jesus! Save her, Bruce? It… this is a machine. IAPTCS isn't alive. There isn't anyone to save," worry started to peek through her expression, "Just a machine running wild."

Bruce couldn't tell if the look was for his safety or sanity. "But a complex machine. One with all sorts of safeguards. We should be able to go in there and pull the plug." Excitement crept into his voice, "We could then find out what went wrong. And safeguard against it the next time."

"Can it be turned off?"

"If not through the computer network, then manually with ease."

"You're sick. You want to risk death to save a hunk of metal." Nancy knew to do it manually, he would have to disconnect the feeder lines. In space it could be done with ease, but in the presence of air it was a volatile operation. "You're not going to try it. It is foolish to attempt a manual override. Hell, that thing makes its own fuel. You are not even sure how much it has."

"Don't worry, I'll try a bypass first, that will unbalance the plasma. I'll be far away if I must break the line. If one of the fuel tanks blows, the magnetic bubble will go too. Much too fast for the plasmatic fluid to degenerate. We can't allow it to happen, Nan."

She stood looking him in the eye, a long silent time elapsed. It was like being in the cavern again.

Bruce felt himself spinning. Shit, why did they send her? He knew why. They wanted him body and soul. He walked quickly away from her, before either of them could say more. Men in quilted vests darted from place to place, laying charges as they went. Two of the tents were broken down. A navy bird loaded the control equipment. The beat of its blade sang of springtime through the balmy air. Beyond, the crater bubbled with deep blue water. Its size had double in the few hours since Bruce had been here.

Bruce arrived at his tent to Ken waiting.

"Thanks for getting me chewed out by the commander. But I convinced him to let me go back down."

"Are you sure it wasn't an order?"

"Are you serious?" Ken laughed. "I'd gladly do time in a stockade than go back there."

"Then why are you going," Bruce pushed, "this is for all the marbles. Hell, I'm the expert so I must go…"

"You need someone to steady the wheel. Down there I would not trust all this high-tech bullshit completely."

The men exchanged a nonverbal thanks. Each sensing the other's spirit of duty and courage. Nancy interrupted the two, warning against heroic fantasies.

"Let me go over my procedures," Bruce began detailing as the trio left. "First, I'm going to cut the laser oven. That device superheats one fuel element so it has its own gravity field. Second, I will oversaturate it with hydronium from the standby converter. Third, is to feed all energy to the polar phase selenium rings. The bubble," Bruce stopped at the entrance to one of the copters.

Nancy held his hand tight. Trembling. The bell hung ghastly like some gallows on judgement day.

"Fourth, I trip the vacuum shut-off bypass, and hopefully, not the delay fuel charges."

She hugged him closely and ran aboard the bird. She didn't want to hear anymore. Then she turned right back to kiss him. "Please… let it go." The door slid shut and the copter pulled away. She watched teary-eyed as Bruce walked the last mile.

By the time they reached the end of the ramp all the navy birds were off. That is, except theirs. It sat a dozen feet from the crane house. Its rotors causing a slight breeze which made the red charge markers dance.

Monitors still flashed signals to the ship off the icepack. Thirty miles away Nancy was being led to the receiving station deep in its leaden hull. Everything was on automatic, awaiting Bruce's command.

Ken entered Bella first, it was much warmer.

Bruce checked the thermometer function of his watch 81°F. He descended the main ladder and pushed the lock-in code. They strapped down at the boards.

"Lexington… Lexington… 1… 2… 3… Copy," Ken flipped the radio to two-way open.

"Copy… 1… 2… 3… Bella… Bella… Good Luck… Bravo!"

"This time, I'll hold the reins, Cowboy." Ken pushed the manual override, "We are on our own."

Computerized graphic displays painted the scene from the bell's sensors. Bruce concentrated on the sonar image of the sat. The crater was now a boiling lake they had to dive through. Bruce nodded and Ken started Bella out. "Water temperature is 130°."

Ken flipped two switches and Bella nosed under. He could see the diameter of the hole shrinking as they descended. "Water is at 150° and rising," Ken reported.

"Infrared detectors are picking up turbulence," Bruce warned. Bella confirmed his statement with a sharp jolt. Icepacks ripped away from the walls exploding in the primordial sea. "Try to approach the cavern's portal dead center. Keep away from the side." Bruce strained against the control sticks.

Ken increased her speed. He didn't want to waste time. Bella's indicators showed she was diving straight down at sixty feet. The door was another twenty feet ahead and barely twelve feet wide. This wasn't going to be easy.

Bella slammed against one side and then another. Both men rocked in their chairs like an amusement park ride. The sub spun uncontrolled into the subterranean sea. The cavern had grown immensely. Mountains and islands had formed out of the ice. The sea Bella now sailed in was not as rough, though strong currents still pulled at her. Ken cut in electro-stabilizers. Bruce marveled at the purple haze atmosphere. Cloud formations of mainly hydrogen gas drifted by white and fluffy. Lightning struck out of the dark sky.

Bruce activated three panels; he changed his screen. Locking in on the black box signal, "IAPTCS has been a busy little sucker. I wonder what she is up to. She has been dancing down here, down one hundred twenty meters, I'll feed you the plot, Ken. This pool is also sixty feet deeper now."

A blurry red image focused to a solid white stack and deep red avenues in faint pulsations. The 3D image matched exactly Bella's position in this nightmare. Ken followed the red path charted by the sub's computer system. As he maneuvered through this new world, violent eruptions opposed their intrusion. Ken wished he had some idea of what was happening. His topographic map led him to IAPTCS sitting passive on a clouded throne. The black waves crested far from the satellite. There were powerful cross-currents throwing chunks of ice into the abyss beyond. Some of the ice was twice the size of Bella. They circled IAPTCS at the base of the water flume.

"There she stands at a plus sixty-three degrees thirty-foot-high wave. Swim up there and click her off. I'll wait for you here." The joke died cold.

Bruce was busy at the computer console. "I think my time factor could be wrong, looks like IAPTCS might come apart in two hours… or less."

This statement met unearthly silence from all sources. They sailed Bella around and up the watery mountain. Spiraling endlessly to the prickly burning cloud. At the top they stood motionless, looking up at IAPTCS's powerful gleaming body. At their side, utter blackness.

"Bella has some booster jets in her underbelly."

Ken wasn't sure if Bruce was asking him or telling him, but he started up the four compression engines. "When you are ready I will open the jet ports."

Bruce gave him a half nod. The sub rose smoothly off the wave top into the eerie cloud ten feet above. Everything was all black for a moment then IAPTCS stood before them. "The cloud must be made of antimatter particles," remarked Bruce. He was trying to make sense out of the weird environment.

Snowball crossed its last snow dune onto a newly formed graveyard. The twenty men poured out of the tractor. The sky was overcast, and a fine light dusting of snow hung in the air. They approached the hundred-foot rocket assembly stretched out in the sparkling snow. They went to work in small teams. A few on the rocket, some on the equipment the tractor carried. All of them oblivious to the Russians frozen in their tracks. The mounds that were their support vehicles dotted the area.

Within minutes the crew had stripped the vital guidance equipment from the rocket. They also removed the lethal warheads and arming device and lay them in the snow. Snowball's crew finished constructing a supersonic rocket cruiser.

"This thing is just a little bigger than my Lincoln," quipped the pilot.

They loaded the rear hatch with their proof. The stubby winged aircraft blasted fire from its tail. Streaking down the snow and into the sky the plane roared out of sight. Minutes later it would rendezvous with a bomber high over the Atlantic. Once, safe in its belly, to be rushed to Washington.

Bruce extended a probe to his black box. He entered a couple of commands and IAPTCS opened like an elaborate jewelry box. Her circuitry was glorious, Bruce thought. It had been a long time since he had seen her computers. Since before her launch. "Now, I go to work," he said with confidence. "First, I'll call up the laser function and shut it down."

Ken looked out the front window at the satellite. On the right side of the generator was a silver soup can, the laser oven.

"Shit! Every time I try to change the laser's condition, I get this stupid, 'D.C. 99' response."

"That means defense code 99," Ken informed him, "it's a common military circuit which fuses the circuits closed." He added, "Usually in the armed mode."

"Well, I can get around that." Bruce did a high-speed search for the defense microchip. It was displayed on the screen, a tiny section of a vast metropolis. He armed the cutting laser. Positioning it carefully, just inches away, he fired at the sat's controls.

On the screen the word, "MALFUNCTION" repeated itself. Then the picture changed to another mini city in the sat's miles of circuitry. "REROUTE SUBSECTION RED A. COMMANDS REQUIRED"

"Here they come, baby," Bruce whispered. His hands moving lightning fast.

"CONDITION IMPOSSIBLE"

"Oh, Hell!" Bruce exclaimed.

The CRT showed a globe with bright and dark red masses shifting about. Black lines dissected the configuration like snakes crawling across the screen.

"The plasma is already unbalanced." He continued aloud, for the record, "The bubble is reflecting laser waves. Shutting down the exothermic process is impossible. Trying to overload the endothermic system." A few more keystrokes from Bruce and Ken's image changed to the aft section. Flashbulbs popped outside the portals. Structures like steel spikes ejected from IAPTCS's body.

"PHOTO-GRAVITY INTERLOCK ENGAGED"

Bruce studied the display before him. Under its message the fuel feed system was fully mapped out. The red laser button throbbed relentlessly. A gentle tap, another block of microcity vanished in smoke. The river of fuel it once controlled ran free. The laser oven turned white hot. "Let's move!" cried Bruce.

Ken snatched the ring, setting the individual retractor motors in operation. The metal threads whipped through the cavern as the sub awkwardly avoided collisions. The two men felt themselves gaining weight as they raced to the surface.

Bruce strained to speak, "I've grounded … the bubble energy… fragmented … overrun… blowout."

A brilliant blue disc streaked out of sight. Its sound could be felt rolling through the maze. Bella sprang from the tumultuous Antarctic sea. The crane, helicopter, and equipment racks bobbed madly on the pontoons.

Ken steered towards the bird. "Start breaking out," he said.

But Bruce was unable to respond. He had passed out from the bends.

Ken pulled a pressurize lever to quickly open the hatch. A whining scream echoed in the transforming desolation. He pounced back into Bella's cavity with a harness. Moments later, the bird was speeding from the site, Bruce being sucked up in her claws.

Wonder how large a dose we took. Ken pushed the notion from his head. His eyes fixed on the tiny aircraft carrier ahead. He pushed hard on the throttle. In the side mirror was a picture of the boiling cauldron's menacing power.

Bruce groaned and tossed in pain. Slowly sitting up he unstrapped himself, "Did I pass out?"

"For about a minute. Some ride, huh?"

Bruce slid into his chair.

The ship waited, its black mouth flickering landing signals. They looked back one more time as a blue funnel appeared, a shimmering tornado that split the bleak gray surroundings. It seemed unholy, a specter.

This was it. *Now, we're turned to dust and scattered across the wind,* they thought. And they waited.

Diving towards the blackness, each man held his breath tight. Guarding it. Loud metal doors slid over their heads, closing out the sky. The helicopter landed with a jolting impact. They sat motionless. Finally, Ken's hand snapped off the engine. Time was unreal to them. The sound of hydraulic pumping its thick metal doors apart rang in the bay.

Nancy broke the bubble. Although she seemed to be in the same state of shock Bruce and Ken now suffered. "You're clean! No contamination! Did you see it?!"

Bruce dropped down from the copter, visibly in pain. Nancy caught him. "Some show we put on," he said.

"I'll say." His voice had comforted her. She continued, still excited, "Lasted five minutes and eighteen seconds. We blew some recorders, but it was definitely subatomic."

"That's good," Bruce received another helping hand from a crew doctor. "Did you get IAPTCS' gravity meld, Nan?"

"Yes. Amazing stuff, it's being analyzed right now."

Bruce was still in the sickbay recovering when Com. Thomas handed him a letter. It was an urgent appeal to go to the White House. Signed by the President. "A jet is warming up now.

Nancy will be ready shortly," in an unknown tone Com. Thomas added, "well done."

"Close to it," Bruce quipped.

Minutes later they were high above the clouds once more. Things were still moving much too fast for Bruce Wells. He needed time to think. To organize the events that had transpired. Even the couple of hours in-flight didn't offer a break. Too soon, he was smuggled into the White House. In an office, in the East Wing waited the President, a senator, and the Scrambler.

The President started, "Mr. Wells, I'm sorry that the times are as they are. You performed a brave and unselfish deed; we all owe you much. But you will soon be in front of the news media."

Bruce could hear the voices of the newsmen in the next room. He gripped Nancy's hand a little tighter.

"I want you to know why you had to do it. As you probably realize it was our interference with the satellite's normal operations which caused the crash. Why we did it is simple... these."

On the desk, parts of the Russian missile were displayed. Bruce eyed them from his chair, recognizing the parts as guidance equipment.

"The satellite was used to create interference. By this time those parts would have been in a Russian missile pointing down our throat..."

"Did you authorize the use of IAPTCS as a weapon?" Bruce incriminated him.

"No," snapped Gen. Wood. "I acted without direct orders." He stopped for a second but couldn't help strengthening his position. "I offered my resignation, but in it I stated my actions were for reasons of national security."

"The Russians already know we have these. They know we used the satellite to get them," the Senator ended abruptly.

"What Sen. Shrine is trying to say is, only the general

population don't know." The President hammered his hand to drive home his point.

"Perhaps they should be told next," Nancy said angrily.

"It wouldn't help," he retorted. "But when we go back to the tables in Helsinki, we will have a stronger position. That is, if we don't let this blow wide open in the press."

"Maybe you've been looking for a solution in the wrong place," Bruce offered, "next time, hold your meeting in Hiroshima. There you will be able to see what the hell you're talking about. The general public should have some kind of control of the things hanging over their heads. I would sure like to see that happen." Bruce rose to face the door.

The rumble of voices sounded like another engine to his weary mind. He tried to prepare himself for another Odyssey. One, that if he had the rest of his life to get ready for, he would still rather not go on. He opened the door to the frenzy conference room atmosphere.

THE END

THE HUNTER

Police lines were set up outside a posh New York hotel, while inside, a man stalked the lobby. Behind him two detectives busied themselves taking notes in disbelief.

"She was definitely here," he said to the skeptical cops. "Let's check the register, maybe I can pick up an impression." The man, Mark, was a thin, out-of-date-looking hippie psychic right down to his beads. His white hair making him look older than his actual twenty-five-year-old, dark mocha face warranted.

The sergeant made an impromptu remark to his friend and partner, a six-two, heavy-set, black police lieutenant, "You think we'll turn up any clues this way?"

"Maybe you'd rather go back to my place for a look in my crystal ball instead," responded Mark, laying on a thick creole accent and giving the cop a smug look.

"He solved sixteen cases this year alone. The Feds swear by his abilities," the senior detective said, trying to make amends.

But Mark was blind to all around him. He placed his hands over the pages of the hotel's registry, one page at a time, slowly at first, with eyes closed tight. Concentration lines cut deep into his smooth features. The veins about his temples, full of blood from many different lines, started beating rhythmically. His bright opal eyes popped open, "this one," he announced, his finger resting on a name.

"She checked out yesterday," said the short, balding sergeant.

"It would appear so," answered Mark. "But I am positive this is the name she used."

"Get that desk clerk over here and show him the picture," ordered the lieutenant. "The room hasn't been re-rented, get some men to go over it carefully." There was a rush of activity as the lieutenant and Mark disappeared into the elevator.

Inside the room, Mark sat quietly in a chair in the corner as a half-dozen pros dusted and snapped pictures of the immaculately clean suite. Several hours passed, it was almost dusk. In that time, he saw the police question everybody on the floor at least twice. The cleaning woman had done the room at 8:00 am, there wasn't a print to be found. And none of the guests had noticed the fugitive occupants either.

The desk clerk noticed one difference, the girl in the picture had red hair instead of blonde when she signed. And she had signed for the double room instead of one of the two men she was with. He couldn't see the other woman's face, but what a figure. Nothing else about the four struck him as odd.

"We're getting nowhere fast here," said the lieutenant, motioning everybody out.

"I'm not getting any vibes either," said Mark. It was the only words he spoke since entering the elaborate room. "But I do have a feeling we're on the wrong track."

"Can you clarify that?"

"We're looking for a kidnapped victim, but I'm not receiving any negative vibes, like fear, hate, or animosity. I think maybe she wasn't kidnapped. Maybe she is trying to take her old man for the two million."

"It wouldn't be the first time. Want a ride home?" The lieutenant knew the divinator excelled at reading people's motives.

"Nah, I am going for a bite to eat and a walk to clear my mind."

At the door to the hotel the curious crowd had grown. Just before exiting, Mark felt a chill run through him, and he swayed as if on the verge of fainting.

Lieutenant Heart put his hand on Mark's shoulder to steady him. He felt the psychic shudder. "Are you ok?"

"Yeah, I just felt something. I don't know what but something foreboding." Mark continued out the door. Several cameras flashed and reporters shouted questions in the hope someone would stop and give them an idea of what was going on.

Inside, Lieutenant Heart whispered to his sergeant, "stay close to the psychic. We don't want anything happening to the good doctor. He is still the only game in town." Then he stiffened to face the crowd outside.

Dr. Mark Srimad sat alone in a diner off Third Avenue eating a fruit salad. He could still feel the presence of a few minutes ago and it puzzled him. It had nothing to do with the case, he was sure of it, but showing up that way made him wonder. He was suddenly startled by a young muscular Jeff Wade, who plopped down in the booth across the table from him.

"Hi there, Mark, old pal, guess you never thought you'd see me again," Jeff blurted out.

That ice cold feeling ran through Mark's body again. "So, it was you!"

Jeff tugged at the hand of a woman standing next to him. She looked like a goddess with jet black hair, golden tanned face, and a perfect shape. "Sit down honey, this is Linda," Jeff said to the both of them simultaneously.

Jeff was the same as he had been two years ago when he tricked Mark into helping him find some sunken treasure. Still with an overbearing smile and loud cultureless voice. One thing was different; at least he dressed better.

Mark was about to lay into him for even thinking about approaching him after the lies he had told about 'looking for his past' two years ago. But there was a woman present, so Mark began, "what brings you around this time, Worm? Got another brooch your grandma left you?"

"Hey, you still sore at me for that harmless story I gave you last time?" Jeff knew he was, "She was someone's grandmother. And being from the Crescent City, I knew you couldn't resist finding something from your hometown. But hey, this time I'm on the level. I know you don't like treasure hunting, but this is something really big. Only, I'm not sure what it is."

"Forget it! I wouldn't help you if your life depended on it."

"Why not? I helped you. Who'd you think got you that brain machine you wanted?" Jeff's manipulative smile was gone.

He was talking about the spectral image projector that Mark wanted to build. He had been turned down for the grants he needed twice, but when he applied for it last year, he got all the money he wanted.

"Yes, sir," Jeff continued, "that little find made me quite the big man at the Institute. And although you didn't want any part of it, I figured you deserved something for your help. Now, you want to see what I got?"

Mark nodded his head reluctantly.

Linda reached into her bag and pulled out a black, drawstring, velvet pouch. Jeff said as she poured out the contents onto the table, "I found this on a little exploring trip I took upstate."

The psychic shot back from the table as if struck in the

face. Pain surged through his brain, causing him to scream in agony. "Evil! Death! Destroy it, no, get rid of it, Jeff. Take it back to where you found it, NOW."

Terror manifested all over Mark's face, his voice alien and harsh from that of a moment ago. His two uninvited guests were shocked and embarrassed by the outburst. Jeff sat amazed by his friend's reaction at the sight of a little head and a few arrowheads. He admitted, the head was gruesome; blood red face with four horns and fangs, but he had never seen him act so oddly before. He also knew Mark had found all sorts of religious artifacts, good and bad.

Linda looked around nervously, everybody in the diner was staring at them. She placed the artifacts back in the pouch, "let's get out of here."

"I won't go anywhere with that! You go," Mark snapped.

"What's with you, Mark? It's only old Indian junk I found in a cave."

"Trust me, Jeff, get rid of it. I only know that it is full of evil power." Immediately, the doctor jumped to his feet and fled into the night.

Jeff and Linda looked at each other perplexed, speculating what Mark had meant.

Jeff Wade was not a man easily scared. In fact, nothing scared him. As he drove Linda home, she pleaded with him to do as Mark said and forget about the cave. Finally, to put her mind at ease, he agreed. He would return the items in the morning and be done with it.

But the night is still young, he thought after dropping her off, and soon found himself on the road to the cave. His mind could not stop wondering what Mark meant by power. He held the crystalized head in his hand as he drove through the dark mountains of New York. He thought how years gone by the tribes walked through these very same mountains. And how many different theories of how they got to this continent. Many said by boats, but there was never any proof of them building boats large enough to cross the rough Atlantic. Some suggested a trip across the North Pole, but such an endeavor could prove fatal. Then something struck his mind like lightning, Indians were known for burying their dead in communal graves facing west. Yet, he found this head buried alone in a grave pointing north. The thought of an important discovery pressed his foot even heavier on the accelerator.

Mark tossed and turned until he fell out of bed a little past three in the morning. He knew Jeff wouldn't get rid of the head, not if it meant money and fame. In the short time he worked with him he held one opinion; Jeff Wade was a treasure hunter masquerading as an archeologist. Mark felt a compulsive force within him to go into his library downstairs.

The walls of his library were glass-encased bookshelves from floor to ceiling. Mark began a nervous circle around the spacious office. This room was always lit by thirty-six candles which illuminated every corner with some sort of sparkles. His eyes spied the volume he wanted, INDIAN MYTHS AND LORES. Flipping through the pages he came upon the face that haunted this night. It was the face of the devil, the head, the spirit the Indians buried on sacred ground. It was this spirit Jeff was running around with. He had to stop him.

There came a deafening roar to the room, the doors exploded, sending a whirlwind of glass into the air. Mark fell to the floor in a bloody heap. His eyes filled with his blood as he watched the book slowly burn. Pandora's box had been opened.

Mark regained consciousness and in his confusion, tried to get to his feet. He stumbled, knocked over some objects, his arms flailing in the darkness.

"Easy there, you're alright now."

Mark reached out to the woman's voice in the blackness, "Who are you? Where am I?"

"You're in a hospital, you had an accident, and we are doing all we can for you. There's a friend here to see you, Doctor." The nurse took him by his arm.

Mark felt relieved by the nurse's presence. He could feel her warm and smiling face close to his as she lowered him onto the bed.

"How are you, Mark?" It was Lt. Heart. He was near but hidden and obscured from his sight. The thought came to his mind before the Lieutenant's words filled his ears, "Son, it's your eyes. You are blind."

There was a long pause in the room as Mark sat motionless on the bed. He heard a rustling and injected a note in a sober tone, "I know, but I don't need eyes for my job."

"Good. I'm glad to see you're pulling through this," Lt. Heart didn't believe him, but there was nothing he could say. "We are going to really need your talents. In the past three nights three people have died brutally. We haven't one clue or reason why. One upstate the first night, and two on the next two nights. The bodies were mutilated beyond description."

"Please, Lieutenant, I can pick up enough from your persona," Mark waved his hand above his hand. He debated telling Heart about Jeff then decided against it for a while, at least until he knew what to tell him. Finally, he asked, "Can I get out of here?"

"Yes, sir," said the nurse, "it was only your eyes that received serious damage."

Mark didn't want to head home to his empty house. He needed to get used to his new world. Lt. Heart was more than delighted to chauffeur him around town. It afforded him the opportunity to give a breakdown of the city's latest crime wave. Mark decided to head straight for Jeff Wade's house on Staten Island. He had to find out how deep the impulsive archaeologist was involved in the recent homicides.

"Is he the man who was with you in the restaurant?"

"Yes, how do you know?" asked Mark.

"I had you tailed the other night. Lucky, I did. We found you in your study after the explosion. This Jeff character must have been involved in the kidnapping and tried to bump you off."

"Yeah," Mark said absent-mindedly. He was trying to see his friend, get a feeling of him. He felt nothing, even as the ferry came closer to the island, although distance was never a problem for him before. He tried to reach his friend with the help of the spirits but reached an empty blackness. The car pulled up in front of Jeff's fourteen-room townhouse-style home. Mark had never been there before. He had been invited to Jeff's housewarming but turned him down flat. Now he felt a touch of remorse as he heard the lieutenant's reaction to the view.

Jeff had left a note on his door, "gone digging."

"Well, where to now, Mark?"

He didn't respond right away; he was silently mesmerized. "Linda," he answered solely, "she's a friend of Jeff's. Only, I don't know her last name or address. We must find her."

"What does she look like?"

"I'll draw you a picture," Mark held out his hand for the cop's pad and pen. A few minutes passed as the car headed back across the island. Mark handed the lieutenant a rough sketch of the beautiful woman.

Lieutenant Heart winced when he saw the picture, "it will be simple finding her; she's in the freezer." He waited for the information to sink in, "why don't you tell me what's up."

"I'm not sure."

"Ok, let me tell you what plain old detective work has turned up. Your friend shows up. Your house blows up and takes you out of the picture. The first murder makes the news, and the Williams pay the ransom for their daughter."

"So, the Williams girl is safe?"

"No. They paid with crypto, but the girl is still missing. Jeff's girlfriend, Linda, is brutally murdered that night in her apartment."

"Why? It doesn't make sense."

"You heard the adage, 'No honor among thieves'" Lt. Heart said, "Well, they don't like to share either. Your friend Jeff may be a kidnapper and a murderer. And Miss Williams may be on the run with him. Or dead. We haven't been able to ID the third victim yet."

"Jeff is a liar and a scoundrel, but he is not a criminal." Mark told the lieutenant all he knew of the head and finished by saying, "He may have been transformed into some kind of supernatural killer. Or he may be dead himself."

Since the killings had all been at night, the lieutenant suggested Mark get some rest. A guard was placed at the front door and Mark found himself alone in his bedroom. But it was senseless to go to sleep when he had been asleep for the past three days. Instead, he felt meditation to be a more useful activity. He assumed the lotus position in front of the open window. He stared into the western sun and searched out the truth with his inner sight. The night came dreadfully slow. He finally ended his meditation as he felt the last rays of the sun's warmth fade from his face.

~

Lt. Heart rang the bell of Mark's house at 7:00 pm sharp. Mark was dressed in a black-hooded robe and sandals for some unknown reason. The two men filed into the back of the lieutenant's private car. The driver started out to just cruise the lower part of Manhattan since two of the victims had been murdered there.

Mark still found it hard to accept Jeff as a killer, but it seemed likely he was. He couldn't picture him at all, alive or dead, and that troubled him. Lt. Heart had an APB, all-points bulletin, out for him but couldn't actually arrest Jeff on such flimsy evidence. Besides, he may not have been in town when his girlfriend died.

The night dragged on, the police radio in the dash sang out of an unusual night of violence and mayhem. Around 1:00 am a call came from the North Bronx; a woman was witnessing a horrifying attack taking place in an apartment opposite hers. The car immediately responded with lights and sirens.

When the lieutenant arrived at the scene a dozen patrol cars were already there. He flashed his badge and went into the apartment on the third floor. There was a fight alright. Lt. Heart stopped short of the door to the flat, his eyes tearing up in disgust. Parts of a human body were smeared all over the inside of the apartment. The attack was the most violent yet. Blood covered everything in the place. The lieutenant was careful not to destroy evidence as the photographers shot pictures.

Mark remained in the car, refusing to enter the building. He rolled up the window, fear rising inside him rapidly. He buried his eyes in his hands, trying in vain to block out the vision. In the bedroom, sitting in the middle of the bed, the lieutenant's eyes stared terrified at what he saw. The head of a young woman with her eyes plucked out and a name carved into it. Mark's name.

The lieutenant flew down the stairs to his car. In the wall leading away from the apartment was a deep, blood-red gash, perhaps caused by a weapon the attacker carried. "Mark, open up! Please, Mark, let me in." The door opened and the frightened man jumped in, "We got to get you out of here. He's after you. Mark, did you hear me!"

"I know he wants me, but he's not around. I've got to destroy this thing but for the life of me, I don't know how."

They drove back to Mark's house in midtown. Along the way, Lt. Heart put out another call for Jeff Wade's arrest. They still had little to go on, but if Mark was right, Jeff was no longer Jeff Wade. He was now some kind of demon bent on murder and particularly his. They reached the house at 2:15 am and Mark got out. Another patrol car pulled up behind them; it was his bodyguards.

Mark touched the doorknob and burned his hand; his scream of anguish sending the cops into a frenzy of action. Lt. Heart burst through the door with gun drawn. One of the cops grabbed the doctor and pulled him away from the door.

Mark tried to get their attention, then broke out at the top of his voice, "Lt. Heart, he was here! I can feel evil. He was here. He found me!"

"I know," said the police officer surveying the room that looked like a hurricane had been there. He grabbed Mark's arm. "Come on, we got to hide you."

"There's no place to hide from the spirits," Mark prophesized.

"Well, let me at least try."

Mark awoke early the next day in the lieutenant's apartment. The lieutenant had been awake for hours. In fact, he never went to sleep. This case weighed heavily on both men's minds. The decapitated woman was a colleague of Mark's. He surmised that Jeff may have approached her with the crystal head before coming to him. It was an ancient deity known as The Hunter and showed up in many religions to bring success to the hunt or victory in battle. It was also known to destroy the people it helped.

They had to make some moves before nightfall and another murder could take place. At 8:40 am, Lt. Heart rang Jeff's bell, Mark was at his side. Two other officers stood behind them, one with an axe, in case nobody answered. The lieutenant was about to give the order when the door flew open.

"Mark, what brings you here this time of day?" Jeff stood in the doorway with that perpetual grin on his face, nothing to suggest a demonic possession. The smile disappeared as he noticed the dark glasses and scars on Mark's face. "What the hell happened to you, old friend?"

"I had a little accident," Mark said carefully studying the man's vocal tones for a clue.

Lt. Heart reached out and snapped a pair of handcuffs on the surprised Jeff Wade. "Jeff Wade, I am arresting you for the homicide of Linda Durrant and several others. Read him his rights," the lieutenant directed one of the cops accompanying him, the one without the axe.

"This has to be a mistake. Linda is dead?" Jeff's voice shook from the shock.

After hours of questioning, Jeff was placed in a cell on the top floor of the midtown station. Bewildered and confused, he asked himself how the police could have thought he committed the rash of horrible crimes. Moreover, how could Mark believe it? He told them of his digging in the mountains for the past few days, it was an unbelievable alibi, but the truth. He collapsed on the cot weakened by the sudden shock of the day.

"Well, what do you think? Either he doesn't know anything about the past few days, or he's the best damn liar I've come across in decades," Lt. Heart put it to Mark in his office.

"I'm not sure. Maybe it's schizophrenia, maybe he's innocent, I just don't know."

"What does your psychic powers tell you?"

"It's not something I can turn on and off like a TV, you know," Mark chastised him. "I don't get any bad vibes from him though. But think of my powers, as you call them, as if the universe is a big house with many rooms. There are rooms for the living, rooms for the dead, rooms for angels, and rooms for all manners of evil. My grandfather recognized I was a seer, when I was just a boy living in the bayou. My nightmares were caused by me looking into and hearing what was going on in those other rooms. He had the same powers, gifts, curse, just like his mother."

"But you can see the future and the past," Lt. Heart recalled Mark's ability to see things out of time. "Have you tried looking back a few nights to see where Jeff Wade was?"

"There are rooms that are in the past, and rooms that hold the future," Mark's face glazed over with a melancholy he hadn't felt since his grandfather died. "I tried to find a room in Jeff's past or one in his future. I don't see anything. I fear he opened a door and let this demon into our room. And its presence is so big I can't see past it."

"I can only hold him for the night, you know. If there's another murder it will clear him, if not we still don't have enough evidence to charge him. I'll go upstairs to try sweat him some more. If he is the type of person, you think he is, maybe I can use the death of his girlfriend to get lucky. I can't tell my captain we are looking for some ancient demon, or the devil made him do it."

Mark recalled his grandfather's death. He had been present when they tried to free a woman of an evil spirit. She had killed her newborn son in the swamp country and the husband reached out to his grandfather. Everybody died in the cabin when it burst into flames, but not before his grandfather managed to push him out the door just before it slammed shut. He got kicked out of seminary school the next day. In a place full of spiritual lore, it was obvious that no religion wanted a seer in their ranks.

He started feeling a bit uneasy. He left the police station and walked down the street. As dusk approached, a driving urge quickened his pace. He had no idea where he was, he only knew it would be night soon. He smacked blindly into the huge metal door of the Institute. His hands groped the portal for recognition. His fingers found the electric biometric identifier panel and a click told him the door was open.

His actions became clear to him for the first time. He ran down the blackened hall of the building which held his baby. The elevator at the back took him down to his lab in the basement. The giant machine all but filled the room, its two eight-foot viewscreen hanging high above the twin control panels. Mark sat in one of the chairs and began flipping switches, spinning dials, and pushing buttons. The machine hummed to life.

Lt. Heart questioned the archeologist over and over about his activities of the past week. He described the way Linda's body had been dismembered. Asked him what kind of weapon he had used because the coroner could tell if she had been attacked by a wolf or a bear. And what had he done with her internal organs. None of it had the desired effect.

He was about to leave when Jeff let out an inhuman groan. He couldn't believe he was witnessing what was taking place inside the cell. Horns pushed their way through Jeff's swollen temples. Fangs grew from his agonizing mouth, and his face twisted, taking on the resemblance of a boar's head. His hands shriveled into claws and his feet became hoofs.

The lieutenant drew and emptied his revolver into the beast that was once Jeff Wade. The monster reacted by tearing his cell door off and hurtling it at the lieutenant, embedding the iron door and Heart in the brick wall.

Police responded to the shots from the detention floor by the score. They froze in shock at the creature which stood six feet tall and rotting before their eyes. One officer shook himself free of his amazement and fired a shotgun blast dead center. The rest of the cops fired at will into the little cell, but bullets didn't faze the demon which hissed and leered at them. Without warning, the creature turned and crashed through the foot-thick brick wall, landing with a loud thud on the pavement five stories below. In moments, it disappeared into the night. A strange warning went out over the police radio for the creature, "Report and wait for assistance. Do not engage alone."

Mark concentrated on the figure that had been haunting his every moment since seeing the crystal head. The figure appeared on the screen above his head. Mark twisted in pain when making contact with the demon. He tried not to move too much so as not to pull out the connecting wire attached to his head and chest. With deeper control, he pictured an old church on Fourteenth Street. He held the picture on the viewscreen as the pain increased exponentially in his mind. His own image appeared at the altar.

The radio screamed in every patrol car in the city, "Creature sighted at St. Luke's on Fourteenth and Third. All units move in."

Within minutes the block was surrounded by SWAT teams and all sorts of cops. Over a bullhorn someone gave the order to open fire, and an unrelenting barrage of fire power ripped the night air apart. The police bombarded the condemned church with flash/bang grenades, setting it ablaze.

Mark felt the incredible force with which the demon

attacked his image. He was nearing his breaking point when he felt something hit him like a ton of bricks. He could stand no more and ripped the wires out of the console. The screen went blank. Mark collapsed, hoping he held the monster in place long enough.

The old church could not withstand the heavy bombardment by the New York police. Its roof and walls came crashing down on the monster, burying it in hallowed rubble. The police made no attempt to find out if the monster trapped beneath the church was actually Jeff Wade or not. Nor did they give any reason to the press for the use of heavy artillery against the mad killer. The city quickly paved over the site. The block was designated as a landmark and a memorial to those who lost their lives to the New York Butcher. The case was closed.

THE END

TWISTED CHRISTMAS

The howl of the icy wind blows the door of the one-room cottage wide open, dumping a foot-thick carpet of snow across the floor. The door slams shut.

"Kris, I think you picked this God-forsaken place because it's so cold you thought I wouldn't dare show up here," says the tall, thin, young man in a midnight-black silk suit, scarlet tie, and mirror-shining leather loafers as he shakes off the snow from his slick black hair.

"And yet, here you are," says the boney, old man, not looking up from his scroll, undisturbed by the rush of arctic air which sends his shoulder-length white hair into a frenzy. "Well, take a seat, I have work to do and no time for your frivolity."

"Don't be like that. I travelled all this way to see you." The man snaps his fingers, and a plush high-back velvet chair catches him as he falls back. He smiles, "Let's do something about the atmosphere in here. I don't want you to catch your death of cold." Another snap of his fingers and the hearth behind the old man roars to life, spreading a sea of flames throughout the single room hovel, melting all the snow instantly, then receding back into its proper place. "That's more like it. Nice and comfy, wouldn't you say?"

"I was just fine before you arrived, Satanael."

"Oh, come on, Nicolas, why so formal? Just call me Satan, all my friends do," laughs the devil with a sparkle in his eye. "And I'll call you Santa, like all the kids do. Hey, want a drink to warm the innards?" Two glasses of dark-red liquid appear on the old, weathered oak desk between them.

Santa ignores the offer as his eyes rapidly scan the aging scroll. He finishes the one in hand and moves to the next, drawn from the piles surrounding him on the desk. Letting it unfurl to the floor, he responds, "you know I only drink milk." He winks imperceptibly, and the two liquids turn white just as his companion is about to raise the glass.

The devil's drink returns to it bloodlike hue as it touches his lips. Swirls of red and white mix in the glass until it is consumed. "Well played, old man. You almost got me." He grabs a scroll from the pile, "Come on, take a break from the whole checking-it-twice to find out who's naughty or nice. What has it been, like a thousand seven hundred and forty years now? Has anyone made the naughty list?"

"I know of one."

"Ouch! Santa, that wasn't very jolly of you." He puts his glass down and it refills with the crimson liquid. "Besides, I don't count. Never been a child. Never been human. Okay, sure, you lead one small coup, and BAM!" His fist slams down on the desk, causing the glasses to bounce up. "You are cast down forever. But hey, I don't have to tell you, right? You do a few good deeds for some kids, and He tricks you into becoming this SAINT. Now, you are stuck, for eternity, breaking little brats' hearts, who ask for puppies every year."

"It's a bit more than that," Santa reaches over and takes the scroll from his hand, "and you know it. Besides, why should I complain, Lucifer, about doing what I loved in my life."

"What did you ever do to become a saint?" Lucifer asks with a hint of mockery from his serpentine tongue. His black wings push over the chair as it transforms into an old hickory stump.

"I gave my fortune to the poor and travelled the country helping the sick."

"All you rich guys do that," snickers the devil, "now we call it tax evasion. And the money was not even yours, you did not earn it, so you gave away your daddy's wealth. Overcompensating, or guilt trip? But really, how many people did you actually help?"

Santa strains to his left, past the devil's wingspan that almost fills the tiny space, to look at the only other piece of furniture in the room, a grandfather clock in the corner. The glass in the cabinet is frosted from age and the brass weights tarnished black. The tick of its movement is barely noticeable in the silence between the conversation. He gave the question another tick then replied, "It's more about the kindness you show others than the material things one gives up. But there is one account I am immensely proud of; I saved three sisters from being sold into slavery by their father when he could not afford a dowry for them to marry. I provided the dowry, thus saving them from a life of prostitution and misery."

"Saved them," the devil glances over his crimson shoulder at the clock, "I'm not keeping you from something, am I?" He smiles, his teeth as yellow as the early moon and continues, "no, Kringle, you just made them slaves to one master instead of many. How many children did the three poor sisters produce? That's what you're really in this for, making sure there is a constant supply of wide-eyed greedy little beggars to worship you. If you really wanted to help those girls, and if I were you, I would have killed their father and set the sisters free to pursue whatever life they wanted."

"Then it's a good thing you are not me." He picks up

another scroll and gently unrolls it. "You know I don't seek fame, fortune, or praise. But I do take pleasure in seeing the joy others feel, if only for a day, a moment. But this is the concept that you, after all these years, down through the centuries, still fail to grasp. That a single moment of joy can last a lifetime for a person who needs just one minute of happiness. One good deed can compensate for an otherwise inescapable miserable existence. I don't take credit for bringing that to them, but I am glad to be a conduit of it."

"Really, one thousand seven hundred and forty years?" Lucifer rises onto his hairy goat legs and spreads his leathery, black wings, the tips touching each wall on either side of him. The bonelike spike at the main spine pokes into the thatched roof. He stands eight feet tall on a three-foot old rotten hickory stump. "Hey, I bring a lot of people joy. The kind that lasts more than a minute. Okay, maybe only five or ten minutes before shame and loathing sets in, but happiness, nonetheless." He continues to chide Santa, "and where are all your little elves? On strike, or laid off, I suppose, it's so hard keeping a decent work force in these trying times. And speaking of work, when was the last time you made a toy? Do you know what kids want today? Not those lame old dollies and wooden soldiers, no, sir, they're into Rampage, Call of Duty, GTA, and Fortnite."

Santa casts upon him a scornful eye.

"Hey, I'm not complaining. Mom and Dad are plopping those kids down in front of the screen, handing them an electronic mayhem device, and turning out precious little maniacal murders in waiting. I just sit back and reap the carnage they sow. Makes my job so much easier."

"Has it occurred to you these kids are taking out their aggression and frustration in a safe and fantasy environment? So, the majority will never pick up a real gun and harm another human being."

"I like that," Lucifer folds his wings back and begins to

pace in the tiny cabin. "Did you give that line to the manufactures? Really, it is a nice selling point. You don't mind if I use it the next time Little Bobby goes to school and mows down a couple dozen classmates." He grabs another scroll. "You really don't have any naughty kids on these lists. I could rattle off a few hundred without even trying. I'm not talking the obvious, Hitler, Stalin, Mussolini, or the more recently dearly departed, Osama bin Laden. No, I'm talking your John Wayne Gacy, Ted Bundy, and Bill Gates. Did you bring them Christmas presents?"

"Bill Gates, really?" Santa looks at the devil and shakes his head.

"Hey, you don't know the guy like I do," Lucifer returns to his swatting perch on the stump. "You think that guy got to where he is today by playing nice? Come on, Saint Nick, you've been at this a long time. You see a lot of good boys and girls go bad. You ever asked yourself, *'Is it my fault?'* You ever say, *'If only I had given him that pony when he was six, he would not be trying to rule the world now.'* You got to know a lot of these failures rest on your shoulders."

The chandelier hanging from the apex of the house begins to gently sway. It comes from an old wooden wagon wheel with twelve spokes, each an arm's length, and in the outer wheel at their end is a bored hole holding a plain white wax candle. From the flicking of the flames in the fireplace and the swaying glow of the candles comes a dancing image of two men locked in deep thought.

The shadows move quicker and become more intense as the devil works up new torments for Old Saint Nick. His mind races over the years, trying to find something he did, something he said, that will tarnish his reputation. He wants something that will make the old man question his faith and what he has become.

A smile comes to his face as he realizes it is not about what he has done. "For a person not seeking fame, you sure did acquire more than your share. You even pushed JC out of his own celebration. And I know how you did it. Coming to America with those Dutch fanatics in the eighteenth century. That was a stroke of genius."

Santa lets the words fall hollow, unwilling to fuel the devil's rage, but it won't stop him.

"When was it, December, sixth, 1773, when your Dutch patronage gathered to honor you. It was a big deal in the New York papers. And when they did it again in 1774, it was all that you needed to be off and running. Before long, the name Sint Nikolaas and Sinter Klaas was all anyone could talk about. Oh! The carvings and paintings of you, well, not actually you, but what people wanted you to look like were everywhere. Carrying your sacks of toys and fruits. And that fool Washington Irving naming you the patron saint of New York in 1809. New York, the most godless place on the globe, and who would preside over it, good ol' Saint Nicholas, the patron saint of Avarice."

The devil is overwhelmed with himself as the room grows darker, smaller with each word. He knows Nicholas has nothing to do with how his image and popularity grew over time, but grow it did, and not always in a positive light. "Oh, yes, those sacks of goodies. That's how you did it. Bribery and huckstery, that is your claim to fame. All those stores advertising how many days to Christmas. How much more there is to buy. By the middle of the nineteenth century you had replaced poor old JC as the reason for Christmas. Throngs of children and their parents lined up in stores to see the real live Santa Claus. And don't get me started on those bell ringers."

"The Salvation Army," Santa looks up from another one

of his lists. Breaking his planning to counter the attack. "Beelzebub, they are good people. Raising money to provide Christmas meals for those who would otherwise go hungry. They are carrying on the work I dedicated my life to, a much-needed job in difficult conditions. Always with a smile on their faces and a song in their hearts. I am proud they take even a small part of my spirit for themselves. And it is that spirit which encourages others to give a little of what they have to help those who have even less."

"An army of drunks and derelicts is what they are," fires back Beelzebub. His goat's head with long curved horns slashing at the wheel above. A swarm of flies rises from him and circles the candles' flames before irresistibly being drawn in. "Their incessant clanging of those bells just to feed their own habits. Every unemployable miscreant in every city cannot wait to don a red suit and collect for charity. Ha! More like hoping to get enough for their next bottle."

~

The devil once again takes the form of a sharply attired businessman, his Satan persona. He shoves the stack of scrolls off the desk and sits on the edge with his glass in hand.

Santa gives a, "Hmph," as he begins collecting the dozens of six-inch-wide scrolls. "A little care, please. I do like to keep things in order around here."

"Why are you keeping lists anyway?" he asks. "That whole making a list and checking it twice came from a poorly written poem. I don't know why people even like it. If I were you, I'd sue Clement Clarke Moore right out of his frock coat."

"Sue him, what in Heaven's name for?" asks Santa. "That line wasn't in his poem."

"An Account of a Visit from St. Nicholas, ha," scoffs the

devil, "he didn't even produce a good title. 'Twas The Night Before Christmas', that's the money maker. But I digress, his description of you, *'a right jolly old elf'*, *'a little round belly'*, *'that shook when he laugh'd, like a bowl full of jelly'*. Obviously, he never met you. I've known you for centuries, I never heard you laugh once."

"Perhaps, you are not that funny."

"Really. I have a joke for you. Rosy checks and cherry nose. He makes you out to be some kind of circus clown. Now, you have to live up to that image."

"It is an image I find amusing," Santa finishes stacking the scrolls, "but the children like it. Their mothers and fathers read it to them year after year, and they get so excited about the coming of Christmas. It is a very nice poem. I really like the eight tiny reindeers' part."

"You are a simpleton, aren't you?" Satan sends the scroll flying into the fireplace with a wave of his hand. "Here you are, a saint, someone to be revered and respected. Instead, Moore turns you into an elf whose only job is that of a delivery boy. Someone who comes around once a year and is quickly forgotten in the all-consuming greed that you bestow."

Santa reaches into the flames and pulls out the few scrolls that landed there. They are smoking but unburnt. He restacks the pile neatly on the desk and points to the plush high-back red velvet chair of Satan's liking. He speaks in the same even tone, but his words carry a much heavier message, "If you cannot control yourself, I will have to ask you to leave."

The devil slumps in his chair like a misbehaved school-boy. He notices Santa's eyes on the clock behind him and is rein-vigorated. "I am beginning to see I misjudged you, Nick. Man has always made light, no, misrepresented us, for their own purposes. Take my situation for example, I'm credited with intro-ducing Adam and Eve to sin."

"You mean, seducing them. But what does that have to do with me?"

"Everything!" Satan leaps to his feet. "Just follow me for a moment." He walks around the desk and stands beside the fireplace. A smoking pipe appears on his lips, "Join me in a smoke? Oh, that's right, you don't smoke, another of Moore's lies. Back to Adam and Eve. The Big Man creates Paradise, right? Gives these two all they could ever need or want. And just before He takes off to parts unknown, He tells them, *'Don't eat from that apple tree.'* Now, come on, me, you, those two poor souls, all we can think about from that moment on is, *I wonder what those apples taste like.* They had to have one, I had to know what eating one would do; it was a setup. The Big Fail, a huge part of the Master Plan. I could kick myself for not seeing it. They eat the apple, and me, I'm reduced to a snake. A Snake! I was God's most beautiful creation, and man paints me as a snake. And you know what the worst thing is, in the end? it was just an apple."

"I do believe it was a serpent. You are giving snakes a bad name. But, again, what does that have to do with me?"

"Are you kidding me," he says as the flames rise in the hearth, "Original Sin! If it wasn't for me, there would have been no need for your foot-washing freak Friend to be born. And you, my dear, sir, would have no job. You'd be a nobody. Less than a nobody... you'd be a never was. But I'm onto your game. I am hip to all you guys. You're in it for the fame and fortune. Look at all the stories being told, the movies..." he blows a cloud of smoke into Santa's face. "Like Miracle on 34th Street, that load of BS. Where sweet little Natalie Wood believes she meets the 'real' Santa Claus. And let me tell you, Gwenn won an Oscar for playing Kris Kringle? they really lowered the bar that year. And you could have set the record straight then. In fact, you can do it anytime you like, just show up at that homage to American materialism, the Macy's Thanksgiving Day Charade and say, 'I'm the real Saint Nicholas and I look nothing like that fat tub of lard in the red suit.' All the world would see you for who you really are, not some toy-shucking buffoon. Although, I will say, you could use a little… no, make that a lot of fixing up. The years have not been kind to you."

"Well, Mephistopheles."

The devil transforms into a red, emaciates figure in a ragged red cape with a head of swarming flies, blazing white light for eyes, two red horns protruding from his forehead, and an uncontrollable forked tongue lashing about.

"You know I can't do that. We are both noncorporeal beings, so photography of any kind is out of the question. I appreciate you may have a problem with your image in the world, but I am satisfied that I inspire kindness and generosity, not greed, as you seem to think. And for the record, the lists of naughty and nice children come from the song, *Santa Claus is coming to Town.*"

As he unrolls another scroll, words write themselves across the parchment. A name and what Santa interprets as a child's wish.

He nods approvingly, "What you think these children are asking for is not what they want. What shows up on my lists are the desires that would make for a better life. And usually, they don't ask for anything for themselves, but for their family or friends who need help. The kind of help that can only come from—"

"Let me see that!" Satan, having changed back, grabs the scroll with the freshly written line from Santa. "I don't see anything here. It's like all the others, worthless rolls of paper. By the way, I don't appreciate you calling me by those other names."

"I see you the same no matter what name you go by."

"That's great! Let's just stick to Satan if you please. Here, I can't read this."

Santa takes the scroll, "Of course not, you have to have

compassion in your eyes. And empathy in your heart. Let me read this latest one to you.

'Dear Santa,

Can you bring my Daddy home? Mommy is always sad and cries a lot. She told me he is on an important tank trip for the glover mint. I know his work must be hard because he wears special clothes in his pictures at work. I know he is good at his job because he is smiling in his pictures. But I miss him, and Mommy misses him. Can you please tell him to come home? Maybe you can give him a ride in your sleigh. He doesn't weigh a lot. Here is his picture.

Thanks Santa and Merry Christmas.'

Santa runs his fingers over the man in fatigues. A tear wells in his eye and rolls down his cheek.

"Let me guess, Daddy is dead. Killed in action. So, Nick, are you going to pull this little girl's father from the grave, drop him down the ol' chimney and prop his rotten, maggot-eaten body under the tree? That will make for a great Christmas present. I'd love to see next year's family Christmas card. Or maybe, just this once, you can get your friend JC to do that little trick He does. You know, what He promised everyone who believed in Him all those years ago. Time for you guys to make good. That little girl is waiting."

"How do you know it's a little girl who wrote the letter?"

"You are as easy to read as child proof instruction, push down and turn. Besides, has anyone ever told you that you speak with the voice of the writer? In this case, I'd say a six-years-old little girl. Quite annoying actually." The devil looks over Santa's shoulder at the blank scroll. "I guess there are a lot of requests like hers. Where's Mommy? Can you find Scruffles? Etcetera? So, how are you going to solve this little girl's dilemma?"

Santa lies the scroll open on his desk and answers with fervor in his voice, "There is a Christmas ornament that she and her father made two years ago before he was deployed. It is a loop-sided papier-mâché ornament with her picture on one side and his on the other. Her mother never puts it on the tree because the memory is too painful. But it will give her mother the strength to tell Angela what happened to father. In turn, it will trigger a memory in the little girl of her Dad, and that she will carry with her forever. In a sense, I will bring her father home to them."

Satan mocks him by bowing an air violin. "What crap! And they call me The Prince of Lies. This whole Christmas thing is nothing more than a scam to make people feel better about their crappy lives. Lift people up for one day, then, BAM!" He slams his hand down on the desk. "It's back to being face down in the gutter the next day. Like all those department store Santas you're so proud of."

Satan sneaks a peek at the grandfather clock and throws himself back into the comfortable plush red velvet chair. He drinks his blood liquor slowly, staring Santa in the eyes. Forcing him to concentrate his attention on him. "And another thing, what about the trove of swine slop, It's a wonderful life?"

"That's not about me," Santa objects, trying to figure out where Satan is going now.

"No, not you per se, but Christmas just the same. George Bailey, an abject failure, a real loser right down to his worn-out shoes."

"His shoes?"

"I was cheering for him when he was about to take a header off the bridge," the devil continues without addressing Santa's question. He either did not hear it or doesn't care. "Then Clarence, the Angel shows up, and the movie goes right into the toilet. Telling him all the good things he did in his life. Saving his brother, stopping that old fool pharmacist from poisoning his customer… but do they tell you how many other people that old coot will go on to kill? It would have been better for everyone if George were never born and they caught that guy after he killed his first customer. And whoever heard of an angel having to earn his wings. Racist propaganda! That's what that is."

"Propaganda? Racism?" Santa ponders, "I don't think you get the nuances of modern cinema."

"Oh, I get it all right," the devil counters quickly, not wanting to lose the upper hand. "That story is nothing more than a rip-off of A Christmas Carol. Another real sorry piece of writing from Dickens. There wasn't even a person named Carol in that story. And three Christmas ghosts; even you have to take offense to that."

"Spirits, but I could see where he was going with it."

"Going with it! Scrooge spends one night going over the success he had his entire life, and because one little boy dies… not even his kid… and he throws it all away. I tell you, I tried… oh, how I tried to get Marley's chains made of gold. Then Scrooge would have happily worn them for eternity. Propaganda! December twenty-fifth is not His birthday. You know it! You Christians go around usurping other people's holidays and traditions. The Norsemen's Yule, where they burned a log for twelve days during the winter solstice feast. And of course, the Roman holiday of Saturnalia at the same time. A good old hedonistic time of food and drink. Also, the birthday of Mithra, the god of the unconquerable sun was on December twenty-fifth. For the Roman, Mithra's birthday was the most sacred day of the year. So, you just stole it. All of it. Racism! Cultural Appropriation! Have you no shame?"

"I don't expect you can understand this," Santa pierces the fake outrage. "All of that is true, but in the early days, Christians were persecuted for their beliefs. So, by celebrating Jesus' birth at the same time as pagans celebrated their holidays, it allowed them a day to rejoice. Sometimes, one day is all that is needed for a person to turn their life around and find lasting peace."

The grandfather clock ticks loudly as if to call to him. The long minute hand rests on the ten and the shorter hour hand is an inch away from the twelve.

Santa continues his defense of the holiday, "Sometimes, that one day changes the world."

Satan also notices the time. Desperation shows on his face. "I know where you're going with this, you are going to tell me about the famed Christmas Truce of 1914. Spare me!"

"Why, because it's true? On December 7, 1914, during World War I, Pope Benedict XV suggested to the warring countries that they have a cease-fire for the celebration of Christmas. Although, no official declaration of a cease-fire was issued, the soldiers took it to heart. Starting Christmas Eve, many British and German troops sang Christmas carols to each other from their trenches. The Germans even had brass bands joining their singing.

"And it didn't end with singing on that Christmas Eve. Christmas morning, some German soldiers climbed out of their trenches unarmed and crossed no-man's-land, calling out 'Merry Christmas' in English. They shook hands, exchanged gifts of cigarettes and plum pudding, and some even played a friendly game of soccer. The Germans lit Christmas trees around their trenches. And more importantly, they recovered their fallen warriors from no-man's-land, where otherwise they would have died and been forgotten."

"Yeah, sweet, they stole the idea from the Egyptians, Romans, and Vikings who first displayed the evergreen trees or its branches as a tribute to their sun gods as he was returning to life. But that would never happen again. No war would ever again take a holiday."

"It only has to happen once to show man's true nature. His desire for peace and love of his fellow man."

"Know what another big day showcased man's true nature?" snickered the devil, "December 7, 1941. I think it's referred to as 'the day that will live in infamy.' You recall the attack on Pearl Harbor; it drew your beloved America into the already raging World War II. The so-called war to end all wars. There was no thought of a Christmas Truce during those times. No cease-fire was ever sought or entertained. It was blood and guts from start to glorious atomic end. And explain this to me, Nick, how come the war to end all wars didn't even slow men down. It has been a steady parade of conflicts, big and small, ever since. Your season of Peace on Earth and Goodwill towards Men is just a thin disguise. Man has no higher nature, no innate goodness. You are all barbarous animals with no more compassion for your fellow man than for a cockroach crawling before you."

Santa cannot deny the truth; man has not lived up to the spirit of Christmas much past the season. In recent years, people have made it more about the material world than the actual reason for the holiday. They have pushed him, or their image of him, out in front of the birth of the Savior. Indeed, some have removed all religious cognations from Christmas and reduced it to a countdown of shopping days. This troubles Santa most of all.

The room grows darker and colder as the devil floods it with his evil intentions. A thick melancholic air fills the tiny cabin in the snow. Satan takes the upper hand in this existential debate over the merits of the holiday. He needs to hold St. Nick for a few more minutes and his deed will be done. The ticking of the grandfather clock thunders in his head like the cadence of the hortator's drum on an ancient galley.

Like a prizefighter, he senses the turmoil he has caused. The pain his words have inflicted show on his opponent's face. He dances around the room throwing jabs, lining up Santa for the final knockout punch. He has to time it exactly right, land one on the jaw, send him to the canvas for the count. Minutes to midnight, Satan moves in. "Face it, Nick, this day has always been marred with the blood of the innocents. Tell me, how many died at the hand of Herod to save your Lord and Savior? That's right! You weren't there, but I was… Thousands…"

"How come every time you tell this story, the number goes up?"

The devil ignores the question and continues his tirade. "And it didn't have to be that way. Three Wise Men, or as I prefer to call them, Moe, Larry, and Curly, God's stooges, because they could have gone back to Herod with the information. God would have protected Jes— Him. Well, maybe, He didn't do such a good job in the end, did He? You know, He always had a thing for killing off sons.

"But hey, I tried to help Him. I had high hopes for Him. Being recognized at birth and given such gifts, I knew He was special. I told Him not to trust His Old Man. You see, by then I had learned all His little tricks. He offers salvation, unending love, but there is always a catch, a string attached. In the desert I offered Jes— Him, dominion over all the nations, a crown of gold, and a jeweled throne above all others. And what did He finally settle for? a crown of thorns and a wooden cross."

"And you wanted nothing in return?"

"Nothing more than what God had asked of me. He wanted me to bow before the likes of you, nothing more than a weak mortal man. No offense."

"None taken."

"So, I told Jes— Him, all He had to do was take a knee. No big deal. I would give Him the world. All would praise Him."

"All do praise Him."

"No! They don't," Satan objects violently, "there are many who don't believe in your Carpenter Son. In fact, instead of His birth bringing Joy to the World, and Peace on Earth, it launched centuries of wars and persecutions…"

Santa holds up his index finger, silencing the devil in mid-sentence. A howl of wind fills the cabin to near bursting. Flames shoot up the chimney and amber as numerous as the stars in the sky disburse in every direction imaginable. The grandfather clock is a single movement away from striking midnight. Santa is gone. The scrolls are gone. The old weathered wooden desk is gone.

Lucifer stands alone in the tiny cabin, his wings drooping to the floor. A look of defeat on his blood-red face stands out in the warm light of the smoldering fireplace. His lifeless eyes sink into the deep pits of his despair. He nearly pulled it off this year. A second longer and he would have stopped Santa from making his rounds tonight. One more tick of the clock, a single swing to the right of its brass pendulum, the only thing left in the cabin to mark his failure, and he would have succeeded.

That grandfather clock chimes in Christmas Day. The Host of Heaven ringing out in the night air. Midnight. Santa walks back into the cabin without the ferocity and elaboration he had left with.

He touches Lucifer's shoulder and transforms him back into the businessman Satan, "Why so glum? It's Christmas, I bring you tidings of great joy."

"Shove it, Nick! I almost had you."

"Well, I did cut it kind of close this year, but you were having such a good time." Santa smiles standing face to face with Satan. "Do you want to know what my personal favorite Christmas is?"

"You are going to tell me anyway, so go ahead."

"It wasn't the Christmas Truce, or the crowning of the Holy Roman Emperor, Charlemagne, which enshrined Christianity in the Western world. Nor George Washington crossing the Delaware River, which I could argue saved the Revolution. It was 1968."

"The Sixties weren't the great times everybody likes to make them out to be," Satan says in an oddly confused voice. "Especially towards the end of that decade."

"Yes, but that Christmas Eve three wise men in their Apollo 8 capsule, Frank Borman, Jim Lovell, and William Anders became the first humans to break their Earthly bounds, the first to view all of Earth, the first to travel around the moon. They travelled the furthest any man had ever gone to show humanity God's creation in all its splendor and glory. On that Christmas Eve, every man, woman, and child finally believed we are one. They ended their night, so far away from home, saying *'Merry Christmas, and God bless all of you, all of you on the good Earth.'* I could not have said it better." Santa wiped a tear from his eye. "I have one last gift to deliver."

"Ah, then I did it," Satan says with gleeful pride, "I stopped you from your Christmas mission after all."

"Not exactly," Santa places a hand on Satan's shoulder, "I have been delivering this particular gift all night. This one is for you. Who else would sit and listen to you rant on this most holy of nights? It is your pleasure to find fault with mankind, to point out his weaknesses, to remind us of all our failures. And you do so, so eloquently. And in doing it, you remind us of how far we have come, to the moon and back, to be better people. Christmas is not about one day in the life of Jesus. It is the celebration of His entire life. His birth, His teaching, His death, and His return to us. It is about God humbling Himself to stand here on Earth, with us, as one of us. He did so to lift us up to His level. It is a celebration of God shining His Light on our world, the whole world, which we were finally able to see Christmas Eve 1968. And for your part in this story, I say to you, Merry Christmas, and to you, a Good Night."

The devil stands alone in the snow. The cabin and Santa

are gone. The stars shine brightly above and a colorful river flows across the sky. The night is eerily still. A warmth enraptures him. He smiles as he starts walking, with each step he sinks a little lower in the thick snow. He monologues, "this year I nearly had him. Next year… next year, I will start with the Slaughter of the Innocents. That will get him." He disappears beneath the blanket of white. "Merry Christmas, Bah."

THE END

ABOUT THE AUTHOR

James L Hill, was born and raised in the Bronx, Fort Apache, New York, in the sixties.

A prolific storyteller, his childhood experiences fed his imagination and later seasoned his novels, unleashing the characters in his head.

Growing up, he believed everyone needed their own gang to go to the store. When asked why he thought this, his answer was, "because the streets were filled with danger, and you needed protection."

He began writing in his teens and in the pursuit of being published, took a paper route, so he could meet as many publishers as it would take to eventually see his work in print.

He later worked in finance and earned a degree in computer programming, his other love.

The combination of talent and knowhow led him to create RockHill Publishing LLC to publish his own work and later give others access to the literary world.

Since starting his company, he has published ten writers, including himself, giving them a voice and platform to spread their creative wings.

James has published in three genres: sci-fi, fantasy, and adult crime.

His sci-fi, ***Pegasus: A Journey to New Eden***, is a thought-provoking dystopian trek through the world of conglomerates and where governments might be headed in the near-future.

The Emerald Lady, first in the Gemstone Series, is a beautifully crafted mythology involving mermaids, humans, and dragons. Followed by ***The Ruby Cradle*** where Zabella is sent to her grandmother, Rehema, the exiled queen, to learn the secrets of the dragons.

Due to his upbringing, is it any wonder James would dip his toes in Crime fiction? His Killer Series: ***Killer With A Heart***, ***Killer With Three Heads***, ***Killer With Black Blood***, and ***Killer With Ice Eyes***, will be his ode to the gangs and mobsters of New York.

Also by James L Hill

The Killer Series - Crime

Killer with a Heart

Killer with Three Heads

Killer with Black Blood

Killer with Ice Eyes

The Gemstone Series - Fantasy

The Emerald Lady

The Ruby Cradle

Science Fiction

Pegasus: A Journey to New Eden

NATURE OF THE HEART

Excerpt

Daybreak that cold December morning came precisely at 5:15. The weatherman predicted snow later in the day and the thick blanket of clouds that covered the skies confirmed it. Narrow straights cut through the ice-encrusted New York streets. The streets and highways were lifeless on this early weekend morn.

Two boys in their late teens and a greying man about forty approached a large, late-model ford station wagon. Each carried a backpack in one hand and a gun case in the other. The boys beamed brightly in the gloom of the deserted dawn. No one but their father, to see their proud, excited eyes darting about. The greying man's face wore no expression of excitement, no sign of joy, just a business-like face. They loaded their gear in through the back and the boys hopped over the seats, their father walked around and slid behind the wheel. The man pumped the gas three times then turned the key, the car roared to life without hesitation. The boy in the seat next to the driver cheered and snapped on the radio. The man turned the heater on full force, shifted into gear, and pulled out slowly.

The boy in the front seat asked, "How long before we reach the mountains?"

"Three hours before we get to the woods. Then a half-hour or so walk in," the driver responded, turning onto the highway's north ramp. There were a few long-distance truckers ripping up and down, but the rest of the highway belonged to them.

"When do we load up?" Inquired the boy stretched across the back seat.

"After we're a couple of hundred feet in," the driver's face livened up a little. "We'll do some targeting on rabbits and squirrels then..."

"When do we go for deer?"

"First, we got to make sure they're up. Then you find yourself a good spot, by a tree or something, and wait. Quietly," his voice dropped at that point, his eyes glanced around the car then back to the road. "Not moving. Your hand on the trigger guard, gun cocked, safety on. And when you see one go by, you throw that baby to your shoulder, hit the safety button and squeeze the trigger. All at once! Don't wait and try to take the safety off first, he will hear it click and with a kick be gone, ploop, out of sight. All at once aim, hit, and squeeze." His face wore a slim, slick smile that made him look even thinner. His muscles drawn tight from the neck up as if he were choking himself. It was an odd smile the boys rarely saw. The steering wheel glided easily through his hands. "Be sure of what you see coming out of the woods. Sit there, let it look at you, you get a good look at him. And when you're sure it is a buck with nice long hat-hangers move like lightning. There ain't nothing alive that will outrun a bullet. Once, one looked dead into the barrel of my rifle but he wasn't out of the covering yet. He took his sweet time in coming to check me out. I waited, waited, and waited until he took about ten steps into the clearing and boom! He spun around and I caught him right in his hind hip instead of his front. He went down, laid there until I stood up. Then that buck tore out of there on his three good legs so fast I couldn't even cock Old Sugar back there." The greying man tossed his head back slightly.

"You lost him?" asked the boy laid out in the back. The excitement running through him like an electric current. His brother and he had been up most of the night fantasizing about this first hunting trip. Now, his father fueled their eagerness with last minute prep talk.

"No," the greying man said firmly, "I trotted off after him. Followed that sucker about half a mile before he started falling on that bad leg. He fell six times before I got close, maybe fifty feet away. The rest of the time, I followed a trail of blood in the snow. Kept hoping he didn't get too far ahead so there'd be something left by the time I reached him."

The boy in the front seat opened his outer orange, goose-down parka and aimed the car's heater directly at his chest. He had been watching the passing countryside growing whiter, if that was possible. Houses came and went less frequently, and farther and farther from the road nestled in evergreens. "Wherever he dropped dead he be there until you got there, right dad?"

"No, not if someone or something gets there first. Besides, I had a job left to finish. That buck was hit, but probably not fatally. When you shoot something make sure you do the right thing by making sure it's dead. Don't leave it to suffer and more likely to be killed by wolves." The greying man drove on looking now and again at the dashboard radio as it faded in and out. "We're not going to pick up much in these mountains. Anyway, there he was, lying about fifty feet in front of me. He stood, trembled for a second, antlers down low, showing its sharp tips. He was snorting, breathing hard and mean. It didn't look like anything you wanted to pet. He kicked one hard time and let loose at me, I cocked, aimed, knocked that safety off and fired all with the same finger." The driver wiggled his index finger in the air. "Dropped him that time for good."

"Danny, where do you think you'll head out?"

The boy on the back seat, the younger of the two by a year and a half, looked seriously at the landscape. He conducted a careful survey of the mountains they were ascending at about 65 m.p.h. They doubled and tripled to the west. Steep inclines broken up by small thick woody flats. To the east there was a thick wooded area which dropped off at points. Finally, he said, "Up there, those peaks to the west, Greg."